Mystery at

Candice Bay

Carin Jayne Casey

This is a work of fiction. While some of the locations are real, the characters, names, circumstances, and dialogue are the product of the author's imagination. Any resemblance to persons living or dead is entirely coincidental.

Mystery at Candice Bay
© 2014 Carin Jayne Casey All Rights Reserved
Published in 2014 by Carin Jayne Casey

ISBN: 978-1-942132-03-5

eISBN: 978-1-942132-04-2

Kindle ISBN: 978-1-942132-05-9

Contact the publisher at: CarinJayneCasey@gmail.com

Credits:

Cover Design by Alane Pearce Professional Writing Services LLC

Cover Art from BigstockPhoto.com
Girl Outdoors #52297750 ©Subbotina Anna; Natural Reserve # 68154910 ©emess; Bike #7499107 ©Gudella

Layout, editing, book design, publishing coaching and project management by Alane Pearce Professional Writing Services LLC **My Publishing Coach.**
Contact at www.MyPublishingCoach.com or by email at alane@MyPublishingCoach.com

Casey, Carin Jayne: **Mystery at Candice Bay**

1. Fiction   2. YA   3. Mystery

This book is dedicated to my wonderfully
independent and precious grandchildren
and their friends. I've learned so much and
I'm genuinely inspired by them.

Also, I dedicate this story to teenagers and adults
everywhere with hopes this mystery will promote
awareness of some serious issues in our world today.

More Books by Carin Jayne Casey

My Dear Rosa Jean
In a beautiful Shenandoah Valley suburb of Virginia, Rosa Jean grapples with a marriage filled with domestic violence, compounded by the abuse she suffered as a child. Her kind Aunt Grace patiently listens to Rosa Jean's story, and together they struggle for her survival, spiritual growth, and recovery.

"... I heard a terrible noise from the living room--a loud thud and breaking glass. I asked myself if something had fallen from a shelf. But I immediately realized, no. I knew from the sound of impact that Brad had deliberately slammed my sentimental porcelain doll collection down, shelf and all. I realized that he must be angry, and there I was, trapped in the dining room. I froze...
It was like slow motion, watching him lumber toward me through the only available doorway; it was sort of like when I was a child walking the train tracks and watching a locomotive meandering toward me."

If a woman has lived in domestic violence most of her life, can she ever really escape or survive it?
And if so, how can she hope to recover?

Granny Babysits the Mischievous Five
Granny loves her five grandchildren, and she looks forward to the days when she gets to babysit all of them. But sometimes Granny gets more than she bargains for. She forgets that these children have very active minds and bodies.

For patien, lighthearted Granny, life with her five grandchildren is always an adventure--and she wouldn't have it any other way!

Acknowledgements

To my children, grandchildren, siblings, relatives and close friends go my deepest gratitude and appreciation for continually affording me with your patience, positive support and especially your belief in me. I am thankful for your unconditional love and the understanding that you freely give me. I believe God has kept watch over me, guided and blessed me along my journey with this story, and I am tremendously thankful.

I appreciate assistance from my granddaughter, acting as my authentication consultant, for my precious husband for his understanding and support throughout my writing, for the wonderful folks at Well Put LLC and Editor, April Michelle Davis, with Editorial Inspirations for their patient assistance.

Especially, it was through Alane Pearce, from My Publishing Coach, and her awesome work and guidance that helped me bring this story to life. I look forward to teaming with you in future novels

Chapter 1

"Casey!" Janie frantically yelled and waved to her friend as Casey climbed the school bus steps.

While Casey had been waiting at the bus stop, her concerns had been how damp her jacket and clothes were becoming from the cold March drizzle, how frizzy and unmanageable her hair would be all day because of this, and, of course, how pissed she was that her older brother, Mark, had not included her in his red Mustang GT—he was going to the same school; why couldn't she sit in the back?

Casey rushed toward the vacant seat beside Janie.

Why's Janie frowning? Could Janie be worried about today's Latin quiz? No, we know we'll ace it. We studied well last night and our homework is ready.

The guys seated in front of Janie mocked her in their usual style. "Oh, Kay-see," they said in a sing-song, high-pitched voice, followed by smooching sounds.

Typical, Casey muttered to herself. *Butch and his buddies are such douchebags.* She stuck her nose high in the air as she passed them. Janie didn't notice the guys; she never did.

Casey looked at Janie's face again. *Gosh, I think something's got Janie stressed out! This is more than about a Latin quiz. Is this bad news? What a morning for it, with me soaked. And my hair! I've got to check it out before class!*

Janie grabbed Casey's arm as she sat, "Did you hear? Tina's missing!" Janie choked up.

Casey was speechless. Her mind filled with questions. *Tina? Missing? What's she talking about? Maybe she's wrong. Where did Janie get this idea? When did this happen?*

"What?" Casey asked.

Janie wiped a tear from her cheek, bit her lip, and lowered her voice, leaning toward her friend. "Casey, Tina didn't come home after school yesterday! Her mother called my mom late last night, and then her mom asked me if I knew anything about where Tina might be."

Oh crap, Casey muttered to herself. *This might be real. What the heck did Tina get herself into?*

Janie hesitated while she quickly looked around. "I wanted to help, but I really couldn't. Besides, I figured whatever I said would be ratting Tina out. I was nervous talking with her mom. The whole thing was just plain awkward!"

"Yeah. Well, what do you think's goin' on with Tina? Do you think she was with Jake and maybe lost track of the time?" Casey could imagine losing *all* track of time if she were alone with a hot boyfriend—if only!

Casey thought about Terry hanging out with her in his folks' old Buick. She remembered how warm and loved she had felt while he peppered her with kisses. She had wanted to go farther with him. *Stop!*

Casey reminded herself, *Terry's with Sheila now, the school slut.*

Janie pulled Casey out of her thoughts. "Casey, I called Jake right after I finished talking with her mother, and he's worried about her, too! He says she's been smoking weed lately and drinking every day. She gets mad at him because he doesn't want to do it. Anyway, he doesn't know where she went either. They did have a fight after school, but not a big one."

Drinking every day; she's an alcoholic! This isn't the Tina I used to know.

The bus doors squeaked open and another student entered. The doors slammed shut while the student seated himself, and the bus moved on.

Janie confided, "Really, he's so handsome and nicer than she is. I will never understand what he sees in her. No wonder they fight! She doesn't deserve him." Her face turned red. "Oh, that was so ugly of me, especially with this going on. Oh Lord, I'm so sorry!" Janie lowered her head in shame.

Oh brother, there she goes again—so sensitive! Casey knew Janie had feelings for Jake, but Janie would never act on them with Tina in the picture.

"Hey, you were just speaking your mind," Casey said. "You hardly ever say anything bad about anyone, and you only said it to me. Don't worry about it."

The bus came to a quick halt at another bus stop, causing the girls to lurch forward while they clutched the back of the seat in front of them.

Casey frowned, "I didn't know about the weed. I wonder where she's getting it. I guess that doesn't matter. It's easy enough if you want it. But I'm not surprised about the weed and drinking. She's been a mess ever since her folks split up. Maybe she ran away. Has anyone heard anything this morning? Maybe she's already back?"

"That's the bad part," Janie said. "Mom called Tina's mother before breakfast, and Tina's been gone all night. Her parents are going to see about filing a missing person's report. Mr. Curtis came over to have coffee with Mom, and when she told him about Tina, he said that while he was heading home last night, he saw Tina and Jake on the street arguing and Tina was crying!"

Casey's mind got stuck on the words: missing person's report. *This is serious! And this man saw her crying.* Janie was still talking, so Casey tried to catch up with the conversation.

Casey interrupted Janie. "Wait a minute. Who is Mr. Curtis?"

"You know him. He's our neighbor, that nice old man who lives two doors down, in the gray house with the picket fence."

"Oh yeah, the one who offered to give us a ride to the library last week."

"Yeah, that's right."

The bus rounded a sharp curve while the girls leaned

to the left, holding on.

Casey looked at her worried friend and filled with compassion. She patted Janie's hand. "You know what? I don't think we need to worry about Tina. She's probably gonna show up today. She's just takin' some time out, that's all. No worries."

Casey wasn't sure if she really believed this or just wanted to support her friend.

Janie sighed, "Yeah, probably so."

"Yeah, well I think Tina ran away," Butch added. Casey and Janie hadn't realized he and his friends were listening, but here they were, leaning over them. Butch licked his lips and looked around, "Maybe she's PREGNANT—you know she and Jake have been goin' at it for a while now. I mean, really hot!"

Casey could feel her temper rising.

Butch laughed sarcastically, and his friends joined in. Another added, "Yeah Butch, I'll bet she had to go hide her big belly before she pops a baby." The boys laughed again.

I can't believe how vulgar they are! Casey thought. *Look at Butch wagging his tongue, like a damn lizard!*

Butch said, "Why not leave? Once her mom finds out, she'll kick her ass out anyway." He kicked up his big black boot in the aisle.

Casey couldn't bear it any longer. She jumped up, leaned in close to his face, and responded in a loud and nasty tone, "Hey *Dickhead*, who asked you? Mind your own business!"

She muttered, "Just give me an excuse," and she clutched her fist.

She turned to Janie with her face red hot and said, "She didn't run away, and she's not even really missing either!" After her comment, the boys turned in their seats, apparently bored with the subject.

Casey and Janie bent down low in their seat.

Janie asked, "Do you think that's it? She ran away 'cause she's pregnant?"

"No, I don't believe it," Casey said. "Maybe she had to get away for a while, with her folks always yelling at each other."

They sat quietly for a moment.

Casey searched for something positive to consider in this situation. She shook her head, "But didn't her dad just get her a car? Things would have to be REALLY bad for her to leave after that, right? Unless . . . did she take it with her?"

"No," Janie said, "her mom told me she didn't have the car."

"Too bad," Casey commented, "police could have tracked her car if it was with her." She immediately cringed for saying that out loud. She knew it could only make Janie worry more.

Attempting damage control, Casey hugged her friend. "Don't worry about it; she's gonna be all right."

The bus made the last stop before heading to school. It took a few extra minutes for the final two students to find seats.

Janie's vision clouded with tears, "Now I wish I'd tried harder to be a friend for her. I knew she was sad months ago! I knew she snuck into her mom's liquor cabinet often, when we did hang out. And I knew she was looking for something to make her feel better. What kind of friend have I been?"

Casey knew Janie was starting on a guilt trip. Then she remembered something. "Hey, wait a minute," she grabbed Janie's hand. "You know when Irene got knocked up and had that abortion?"

"Oh yeah, and Tina vowed that if or when she *decided* to have sex, she'd choose the partner AND use birth control!" Janie paused. "And that was not very long ago either!"

In an attempt to bring hope to both of them, Casey announced, "I hope—no, I *believe*—that whatever's going on with Tina, that she's in control of it and she'll be found."

With as much purposeful sternness as she could muster, Casey continued, "Remember this," pointing her finger. "Not your fault, Janie—whatever happens. And no reason to worry over her being gone—gone for only ONE day."

"You're so right!" Janie said.

They smiled at each other.

Casey sighed with relief, thankful they could be positive about this mess, at least for the moment.

Casey commented, "You know, she was awesome in the church choir. . ."

Janie finished the thought, ". . .before the divorce started."

"Yeah, she had it all together before that."

Casey thought about her own family. She had a kind and caring family, even if Mark was sometimes mean to her, and she realized how fortunate she was for that.

Not everyone had such a loving home.

The bus stopped in front of the school, and the doors screeched open. All of the students quickly unloaded from the bus and hurried into the building.

When they entered the school, Casey and Janie rushed to their lockers. The girls didn't use their lockers much, with so little time between classes, but they liked to visit them most mornings and during lunch to change books.

Casey wondered if she might find a note in her locker. For the past few weeks, she had been finding notes in her locker almost every day. A secret admirer? She wasn't sure if she should be excited or worried.

At first, the notes were exciting because she didn't have a boyfriend anymore. Sometimes the notes contained hearts, and sometimes she found poetry. She would look around and imagine one of the more popular (or most wanted) guys to be her admirer.

But having a secret admirer could turn out to be embarrassing. Casey was trying to figure out the *who*, and depending on that, it could be a humiliating situation. Regardless, she wasn't ready to share this information with anyone, not even Janie.

Casey enjoyed daydreaming, about Steve, a built and sexy senior on the football team. She imagined Steve confessing that he was hot for her. At her locker, for all to see, he pushed himself against her and held her in an embrace. He played with her hair while he looked adoringly into her eyes, and they began to kiss passionately

Casey carefully opened her locker so no one else

could see inside. Yes, there was another note lying on top of her books. Quickly, she snatched it and placed it inside a book so she could read it privately later.

Butch followed the girls so he could remind them of his disgusting theory. "Yep, Tina's in trouble, trouble, trouble," giving a fake look of concern as he wagged his head.

Casey glared at him and showed him her fist.

Butch casually reached for her shoulder. Casey had a short fuse when dealing with Butch, and without thinking, she shoved his arm. She did it much harder than she had meant to. Butch lost his balance and tripped on a couple of books lying on the floor. He fell, his eyes wide with surprise and his face red. His buddies pointed at him and snickered. One of them asked, "Hey Butch, are you fallin' for Casey?"

His friends continued to laugh while they helped Butch up. "Ha, ha. Very funny!" he responded once he had his balance.

While Casey fully enjoyed his humiliation, she looked across the hall to see William, the (disgusting) school janitor, leaning on his mop and watching. When he caught her looking at him, he began to walk toward her. Casey motioned her hand to him and said, "We're all fine here." Thankfully, he stopped. Casey had no interest in having a conversation with this man, and she didn't want to be seen with him either. *He's so sloppy! Why doesn't he wear clean clothes and take a bath once in a while!*

Once he'd regained his composure, Butch muttered loudly, "BITCH!"

The girls looked around for teachers or monitors in the hallway. None seemed to have witnessed the incident—except William. Casey knew she was lucky this time, and she'd better control her temper.

Proud of herself, Casey slowly strutted down the hallway in her short plaid skirt without looking back.

Chapter 2

"This is great!" Casey said to Janie. "What a beautiful day for a ride!"

"You're not kidding," Janie responded.

The girls traveled the bike trail toward town with a gentle breeze dancing through their hair while they basked in the warm sunlight. They rode along slowly so they could ride side by side and talk.

"Casey, if it wasn't for this whole thing about Tina," Janie began, "what would you think about Jake and me hanging out together?"

Casey smiled at her friend, "Janie, you two would be awesome. Anyway, I already know you have the hots for him. And, no wonder, he *is* nice and built!"

Janie smiled timidly. "Yeah. He's the only guy I've ever thought about that way."

"To tell the truth, Janie," Casey paused, "I've always thought he had feelings for you, even while with Tina."

"Really?" Janie perked up.

"Yeah, girl. I noticed him looking you over several times. And he has always gone out of his way to talk to you."

"Casey? Are you still a virgin?" Janie added, "just wondering. I still am."

"Oh, you're really thinkin' about Jake!" Casey laughed. "Yeah I am, but I just about gave it to Terry. Came close."

"Well, maybe it's a good thing he hooked up with Sheila then," Janie said, "I never thought he was being real with you."

"Yeah, I know he's no good," Casey responded, "but sometimes I wonder what it would've been like. You know."

They approached a curve, and Casey fell back behind Janie. They didn't want to collide into incoming traffic that might be around the corner.

Suddenly, Butch and his buddies pushed their way through some bushes and jumped in front of the girls.

"Hey, stop!" One of the guys shouted, and they blocked the narrowed part of the tree-lined path. Casey and Janie stopped their bikes.

"Hi Kay-see!" Butch said in a mocked feminine voice. "Betcha weren't expectin' us, were you?" He and his friends laughed sarcastically. He smiled at Janie and added, "Ah, and here's my sweet little Janie."

Oh Geez! As usual, these jokers ruin a good time. Casey glanced at Janie. *Yeah, and apparently Janie's scared. Thanks a lot guys!*

Casey stood tall and glared at Butch.

Butch grabbed the handlebars to Casey's bike so she couldn't move. "So what're you gonna give me to pass?" He and his buddies laughed, making vulgar kissing gestures.

Janie cowered while Casey presented herself as if totally unafraid. *What do they always say? Fake it till you make it?*

Casey assessed the situation. She glanced around, noting the area was relatively secluded with trees and they were in a perfect spot to be ambushed like this—if that's what it was.

Casey confidently smiled at Janie.

"Ah, Wonder Woman, for sure," Janie said, loud enough for Casey to hear.

Well, yeah, I guess I do have to act like a freakin' wonder woman if I expect to get us out of this mess. It's just these morons anyway. She cleared her throat.

"It's not what I'll give you TO pass, but what I'm gonna give you if you don't leave us alone NOW!" She jumped off the bike to stand facing Butch.

Surprised by Casey's response, Butch let go of the handlebars. Casey's bike fell to the ground with a hard, loud crash. The boys looked around to see if anyone had noticed and backed a few paces away from her and Janie. They didn't want to get into any trouble.

Last week Butch and his friends had been reprimanded because they bullied a shy freshman at school. They had taken his lunch money and smacked him around. Butch and friends had escaped serious discipline because the freshman refused to name them and suffered no injuries.

"I don't know about her, man. Let's get outta here, okay Butch?" one of the guys said.

Another said, "Yeah. I don't want any trouble. My dad's ready to ground me as it is."

But Butch ignored them and didn't move.

While they each stood their ground, Mr. Curtis came

strolling along the trail. Butch and his buddies ran back through the bushes, so Mr. Curtis wouldn't be able to identify them.

Mr. Curtis stopped and asked, "Janie, do you girls need my help?"

Cowards! Casey muttered to herself, thankful that they had left. She picked up her bike, checking it over before hopping back on it. "Nope, my bike fell, but it's all right now."

"Well, I can walk along with you girls for a ways if you'd like," Mr. Curtis kindly offered.

"We're fine now, thank you," Casey said, sounding a tad too prissy.

I don't know why, but I don't like you, old man. I don't care how helpful you try to be. She forced a courteous smile toward him.

Casey could vaguely remember an older man from her childhood who had made her feel uncomfortable. She used to enjoy playing with her friends, Kathy and Timmy in their yard most days, and their uncle would often come out to play with them and give them candy. He must have been about the same age as Mr. Curtis. Their uncle began pulling the girls onto his lap, and while he bounced them on his lap and sang to them, he would hug them real close.

At first Casey really liked him and she laughed while he bounced her on his lap. But then Casey started feeling strange about the way he hugged and touched her. She didn't like it; something wasn't right about it. Finally, Kathy and Timmy's uncle made her feel uncomfortable enough to mention it to her mother. That ended her visits to their house.

Before he proceeded, Mr. Curtis carefully looked around. He didn't see the boys or anything that looked suspicious. He glanced at Janie, and then at Casey. "Well, all right. Be careful."

Janie regained her composure and called back to him, "Thank you for wanting to help us." She watched as he walked farther down the trail.

"Casey," Janie said, "I'm so glad Mr. Curtis showed up when he did."

"Yeah, I know you are," Casey responded, "but I think we could've handled the situation fine by ourselves."

Casey paused, *let's be honest here.* "Well, maybe I'm a little glad too."

Relieved with the incident behind them, Casey and Janie reviewed some of the highlights. Janie shouted, "It's not what I'll give you to pass, but what I'm gonna give you if you don't leave us alone!"

"Yeah," Casey added, "and WHAM goes my bike. Good thing he didn't break or bend anything."

"Or wonder woman would chase him down. Ha ha ha!" Janie said.

They laughed while they rode along the path for a few minutes.

"Hey," Casey said, "do you still want to ride to town, or should we go home and do it another day?"

"Oh, let's just ride home," Janie replied.

"Race ya to the end of this trail!" Casey yelled.

They peddled fast and it looked like Casey would be the winner, but she suddenly slowed down, letting Janie pass. They parted ways at the trail's end.

"See ya later, slow-poke!" Janie yelled.

Casey smiled and waved good-bye.

Once home, Casey spent the better part of the evening in her room teaching Rusty, her reddish-tan Pomeranian, some fun tricks, like jumping through a hula-hoop.

Since Casey's dad and brother planned to help Joey's dad fix up an old car that evening, Casey and her mom decided to eat pizza and chips for dinner.

"So, did you and Janie go to town today?" her mom asked.

"No, we just rode our bikes around the park awhile and decided to go to town some other time."

"That's what I thought, since you arrived home so much earlier." Her mom set the TV trays up in the living room. "Nothing happened though, right?"

"Oh no. Nothing unusual." Casey brought their drinks into the living room. She didn't mention the incident at the park with Butch and his friends, not wanting to worry her mom over what she now considered as nothing.

Casey and her mom settled in the living room for their dinner. They selected a good chick-flick from the on-demand menu. Rusty sat on his living room blanket with his bowl of food beside him.

Casey again thought about Tina and her parents' problems, the divorce, and what Tina's home life must've been like. She wondered if all that caused Tina's disappearance.

Casey realized not all of her friends were as fortunate as

she was. *Oh man, I'm so thankful I have such loving parents— to me, to each other, and to Mark. There's so much warmth in our family! I'd never think about running away.*

She looked at her mother. *It's so nice to have Mom all to myself sometimes.*

Casey gave her mom a big hug.

"Well sweetie." Her mom smiled. "What brought this on?"

"I was just thinking about Tina and her family," Casey responded.

Her mom wrapped her arms around Casey. "Yes, I understand. We are all very concerned." They sat quietly for a moment, then her mom continued, "There is something we can do whenever we feel worried about Tina—pray about it. God hears your prayers, you know."

"Yes, I know that, Mom. I do pray for her. Maybe not enough though," Casey said. Then she silently prayed, *Oh Lord, please bring Tina back safely so her family can have a chance to live a happy life together.*

Her mother suggested they pray together, which they did. Then Casey turned on the movie and took a slice of the pizza.

Slowly at first, Jake and Janie had begun calling each other frequently at night. His heart was tender because his girlfriend had disappeared, and Janie was empathetic. Beyond that, they had always had an attraction towards each other. Lately, their conversations were more about themselves, and much less about Tina. They were developing a relationship.

Jake listened intently while Janie told him about Butch

and his buddies scaring her and Casey.

"Oh my God, Janie. Please take good care of yourself. I couldn't handle it if anything happened to you. There's so much fun and happiness I want for us."

Janie giggled, "I wouldn't have told you about it if I thought it would cause you to worry."

She reassured him, "Yes, I will be careful. I want us to have many happy times together, too."

They both giggled, and began planning things that they would do in the future as girlfriend and boyfriend. As soon as Tina returns, Jake intends to tell her that he and Janie are now together. They both believe Tina will be understanding. Whatever reason she had to run away, it had nothing to do with Jake.

Their conversation had to be cut short, since Janie knew she needed her sleep in order to do well on tomorrow's English test.

"Good night, my sweet Janie," Jake said. "We'll be together soon."

"Yes," Janie responded. "Good night, honey-bunny." And they both giggled again.

They took turns making kissing sounds into their cells before hanging up.

Janie smiled, fluffed her pillow, clutched her stuffed doggie close to her heart, and then she immediately went to sleep.

The next morning wasn't one of Casey's best; she was not a morning person. Mark waited outside the bathroom they shared. Inside, Casey gazed at herself in the mirror, whispering, *Oh baby, you're so hot. Yes*

Steve, I love you, too. She placed both hands on the mirror, giving it a romantic kiss.

Mark knocked at the door loudly. "Come on, get out!"

"Stop! I'll be out in a second," *and thanks for the mood-kill.*

After she finally believed her hair and makeup looked perfect, Casey let her brother have the bathroom. He glared at her as he entered.

Casey glanced at her alarm clock.

She had spent too much time in the bathroom primping. *Oh no!* She fussed at herself for taking so long (again).

Casey gave herself a few seconds to find the tight jeans she wanted to wear, but they were wrinkled. This would cost her even more time dressing.

"Oh, no!" she shouted.

At the sound of Casey's voice, Rusty bounded up the stairs, skipping every other step. Casey could smell the grease from the frying bacon and knew Rusty had been in the kitchen. He had a charming way of begging, and he typically got all of the crisp bacon he wanted.

Hearing that breakfast was ready, Casey and Rusty proceeded down the steps. As always, he started off a few steps ahead of her, then patiently waited for her to catch up, making sure that she made each step safely.

While the clothes dryer worked the wrinkles out of her jeans, Casey quickly ate two crispy pieces of bacon and gobbled down some cereal. She hurried to the sink to rinse her bowl before putting it into the dishwasher.

Wham! Her bowl hit the edge of the counter and

milk splashed onto her red top.

"Crap!" she muttered. *Now I'll have to find another top! Nothing I own is as pretty, or as sexy, as my red top!* She and Rusty rushed back up the stairs to search for another shirt.

What? Am I hoping to impress my admirer? But he might be a jerk! Agitated at that thought, she chose a simple pink blouse. She held it up. *No, it could be Steve! I must look sexy.* So she searched until she found a tight, low cut blue t-shirt.

Casey loved to ride in Mark's red Mustang to and from school when he let her. But as usual lately, his car was in the shop and Casey would be riding the bus. Not fair! She began counting the days until she was old enough to get her license and have a car of her own.

Before walking out the door, Casey's mom called her back to the living room. "Honey, I don't mean for you to be afraid, but at the same time—while we still don't know what has happened to Tina—please be extra alert to your surroundings. Don't let strangers in your personal space and be careful." She lovingly rearranged a few strands of Casey's hair. "Just do this for me, alright?"

How exasperating! Does she think I'm a dummy? Casey shrugged her shoulders, "Yes Mom, like always!" *Duh!* She quickly gave her mother a peck on the cheek. "Don't worry. I love you."

Her mom hugged her. "I love you too, dear."

Casey hugged and kissed Rusty, then shut the front door as she left. He quickly perched himself on the arm of the rocking chair so he could watch her walk to the sidewalk while he yipped a loving farewell.

Although Casey's wait for the bus was only for five minutes, it seemed longer. *Will I be getting a love letter today? Maybe a poem?*

"Hi, Casey!" Janie called to her, when Casey reached the top step on the bus. Casey worked her way over and sat with her friend.

"Guess what happened?!" Janie said, grabbing Casey's arm.

Casey looked at her friend. *Oh my God, she's been crying! What's she upset about now? Geez, what else could be happening? We've already had enough excitement lately.*

"What?" Casey asked.

"This morning I discovered someone slashed my front bike tire!" Janie blurted.

"Huh?" Casey said. "When did that happen?"

"I don't know. Must've been sometime during the night. I noticed it this morning, getting ready for the bus."

What's happening to our neighborhood! Casey wondered, genuinely concerned. *First Tina disappears, then guys we know jump out and scare us, and now this!* She had always believed that folks at Candice Bay were safe to leave their bikes (or other items) in their yard or driveway without worries that property would be bothered. Not anymore.

Casey was about to fuss noting *this was a clear act of vandalism. A crime!* But she didn't want to cause Janie to be further upset, so she attempted to support Janie by making light of the incident.

"Hey, it was probably some young kids, not even thinking about what they were doing or the harm it would cause."

"I suppose so," Janie responded, shrugging her shoulders. They began chatting about their Latin class, seeming to forget about the incident.

Casey continued to think about Janie's slashed tire while the girls walked the hallways from one class to another. Before their last class, she said, "Don't you think it's an odd coincidence that your tire was slashed right after our run-in with Butch?"

Pensively, Janie said, "I thought about that, too, but would he do it? I'm not sure, and I don't want to accuse anyone without knowing for sure."

Casey argued, "Yeah, well. If your parents report it to the police, then it will be the police department's job to investigate and find out if Butch had anything to do with it. He and his buddies should at least be questioned."

Janie refused, saying that she was sure her parents would not want to file a report even if they had known anything about the slashed tire or the incident with Butch.

"You mean you didn't tell 'em?" Casey said. "I think they should know, but I guess that's your call." She held her mouth shut tightly, knowing it would do no good to go further with it.

Janie's parents were still suffering from the effects of living in New York City. While there, they had witnessed several criminal acts committed by gangs, which was why they had moved. They remained fearful and would not want to do anything to bring attention to their family.

Casey decided she should share with someone about the incident with Butch. *I know,* she decided, *I'll tell my awesome brother and Mr. Cool cuz. Who better than them? And Janie certainly can't be mad at me for telling my family. Besides, if she's not going to tell her dad, she'll be needing Mark and Joey to help with the tire.*

Casey paused a moment to think about Mr. Cool cuz. He sure loves the outdoors, especially hunting and fishing like his dad. He seems to enjoy doing yard chores, like mowing. Casey could imagine him happy as a mountain man, living off the land. Since he often lifts weights, he's muscular in build. Yes, Joey's a rough and tough fella, the macho type, but always kind with others in his own way.

Casey quickly texted her brother to see if his Mustang was out of the shop yet. It was.

Once school let out, Casey rushed to Mark's Mustang. She arrived before Mark and Joey, but didn't have to wait long for them to arrive.

"What are you doing here, Casey?" Mark said sternly. "You're gonna have to ride the bus home."

"'Cause we already have plans," Joey finished the thought, nodding in agreement.

"Yeah, I know. I just wanted to talk with you both for a minute," Casey said.

"Sure. What's up cuz?" Joey smiled and threw his arm on her shoulder.

Once she had explained about the incident with Butch, Mark and Joey promised to keep a look out for the girls.

"Hey, Casey," Joey said. "You know I'd be happy to talk with Butch. Anytime." He clasped his fist into the other hand, smiling.

Oh yeah, I know you like to sound rough sometimes. I'm sure glad you're on my side! Casey thought, but she said, "No, I don't think you'll need to *do* anything, not this time anyway." She turned to walk away.

Just as Mark turned on the engine, Casey turned back toward them. "Oh, and another thing, that may or may not be at all related, Janie's bike tire was slashed last night. And she doesn't want to tell her parents about it."

Mark and Joey looked at each other and whispered something before turning to Casey. Mark said, "Casey, tell Janie we'll take care of her tire. No biggie." Then he pulled out of the lot.

Joey waved at Casey. "Yeah, no problem!"

Casey yelled after them, "Thanks!"

That night, Joey and Mark replaced Janie's bike tire. They also chained and locked her bike to a post on the front porch.

"Our heroes," Casey announced, and both girls gave Mark and Joey hugs.

As Janie hugged Mark, he instructed her, "Sometime soon you'll have to share this with your parents." Janie nodded her head in agreement.

Casey was so proud of her big brother and cuz.

I can always count on you both to come to our rescue.

Chapter 3

While Casey ate her breakfast cereal Saturday morning, she listened to the local radio station. She stopped eating when she heard the announcer speak about Tina:

And now for our latest news, we have a missing teen from Candice Bay. The area is being canvassed for the missing teen—a sixteen-year-old from Candice Bay High School did not come home after school on Monday, missing now for five days. At this time, according to Candice Bay Police Captain Webber, it has not been determined if there's been foul play or if the girl is a runaway. The police department has continued the search of Candice Bay area since Wednesday with no definite findings. There's a $1,000 reward for any information regarding this girl's disappearance or leading to her recovery. Captain Webber will be making a formal report on this later today. Be sure to watch the twelve o'clock news.

It was official. Tina was missing. Casey acknowledged. Tina's name wasn't stated and the news appeared to be vague. She reasoned, *they didn't say her name because she's a minor. Maybe the authorities are hoping Tina will soon be back. I sure hope so!*

Casey quickly cleaned up her breakfast dishes and bargained with her mother to let her go to Janie's and finish her chores later.

"Sweetie," her mother said, "wouldn't you like to sit and talk with me about this terrible news?"

"Yes, Mom," Casey replied, "but right now I just want to be there for Janie."

Her mother nodded, "I understand," and she agreed. Casey hugged and kissed her mother, then gave Rusty a loving pat on his head. He then perched himself at the window to watch Casey leave.

Casey rushed over to Janie's house to tell her what she'd heard. Janie and her family had been listening to the news too.

Janie's dad had the local newspaper in his hand. "Well. Let's see what the paper says about this." He opened the paper to the first page and began reading:

> "CANDICE BAY–Police department has issued a statement that Search and Investigation for missing person TinaVanelli is underway. This local sixteen-year-old disappeared from Candice Bay area on Monday, March 4, after school. Please call the Candice Bay Police Department immediately with any information leading to her whereabouts."

Janie's parents hugged and comforted both of the girls while Janie's mother murmured, "I'm so sorry." Tears quietly trickled down Janie's face and Casey quickly grabbed a tissue from her pocket and handed it to Janie, while she desperately tried not to cry.

Damn! Casey muttered to herself, *guess my theory for the radio not saying her name was wrong.* Tears welled up in Casey's eyes and she wiped them away with her hand.

Janie's dad initiated a prayer for Tina's safety, peace for her family, and protection for all of the Candice Bay teenagers.

Casey's head ached while she pondered the situation. *What can we do? Surely there's something constructive we can do to help Tina in this. I know Janie and some others would help.*

Casey asked, "What can we do?"

Janie's mother placed her finger to her pursed lips, "Well, in other similar cases, people put up posters or handouts about the missing person."

"Hey Janie. Let's make posters!"

"Oh yeah! That's a great idea. I have a picture of her we can use!"

Janie's father said, "I want to encourage you, and I'm available if you need me."

Janie responded, "Thanks Dad, but I think we'll get plenty of help from our friends."

"Come on Janie," Casey said. "Let's go round up some others now." The girls left, smiling with happiness to have something positive to do and to know they had Janie's parents' encouragement.

Within an hour, the girls had enlisted some of their friends for their project, using Casey's house as their headquarters. As organized as they could be under the circumstances, each of the girls took on assignments for making the posters.

Sondra announced, "I can print copies of this photo Janie has of Tina. My dad has a great color printer at home that he'll let me use. I'll do that now." Sondra rushed out the door with the photo in hand.

Joyce and Kaye volunteered to buy the necessary materials: poster boards, markers, and tape. "I really think that ol' Mr. Stevens will give us the supplies, once we tell him what it's for," said Kaye. They too rushed out.

Meanwhile, Casey, Janie and a couple other girls stayed behind to sketch how the posters should look, and to devise a plan to get posters out to the entire area as best they could.

Soon the group reunited, and they had a simple lunch break using a couple of pizzas they found in the freezer, and chips and canned sodas from the pantry. Excited and eager to get started, the girls ate quickly and cleaned up.

Immediately they began work on the posters, using the printed photos, supplies, and sketch. While the girls were still hard at work on the posters, Casey took the initiative: "I believe we can cover a larger area if we split up into groups to various sections in the Candice Bay area." She looked at the group. "What are your thoughts?"

Sondra offered, "I'm texting my brother now. I think he'll agree to drive Joyce and me around." She paused a moment, intently looking at her cell for his response.

"Got it! Yes, we have a ride."

"Okay then. Sondra, how about you and Joyce going to the northern area of Candice Bay, and place posters wherever you can? That's mostly neighborhood, but if you know anyone there, maybe you could stop by a few houses, too."

"Yeah," Sondra said as she and Joyce nodded to each other. "We can do that."

"I know lots of people there," added Joyce, "that's where my church is, and most of my relatives." Several girls expressed their agreement, that this area was a good choice for Sondra and Joyce to handle, especially since they had use of a car.

Casey continued, "And Darlene, could you and Kaye walk through the business section?"

Darlene and Kaye smiled at each other. "Oh yes," Darlene said, "Kaye and I will be glad to do that. We can stop and chat with people working most of the stores, too. Maybe they'll also put up pictures of Janie at their counters, and spread the word with their customers."

"And," Kaye giggled, "We all know I'm a good talker." The other girls giggled at that remark, all knowing Kaye is indeed the most talkative of the whole group.

Janie and Casey looked at each other, "Well, I suppose we could handle the rest of the area. We can do using our bikes if we have to," Janie began, "But maybe we can get Mark or somebody else to drive us?" She looked inquisitively at Casey.

"I don't know about a ride, Janie. Mark's with Joey today out fishing somewhere." She put her hand on Janie's shoulder, "It'll work out somehow."

While the girls were hard at work finishing their posters, with some at the kitchen table, some stationed at counter spaces, and others crouched on the floor, Casey's parents came in. They looked around, marveling at how busy the girls were. Once they realized the purpose of the project, they wanted to assist. Casey's dad announced, "Hey girls, if you promise to bring them back in good condition, you can borrow both of my staple guns to attach posters to trees."

All of the girls squealed with delight, and they quickly agreed.

Casey's mother waved her hands into the air, "I volunteer to serve as a driver, so a broader range of the area can be reached than if you went by bike."

Casey held her hand up briefly, "that'd be Janie and me, Mom."

The girls smiled at Casey's parents, and thanked them for their help.

Sondra added, "Oh, and thank you for our lunch!"

Casey's mom quickly noticed the empty pizza boxes, stacked beside the trash can, "Not a problem! We're glad to help." They all enjoyed a group hug.

The posters, each with a photo of Tina, read:

Help us find our friend, Tina Vanelli, 16.

Missing since March 4

from the Candice Bay area.

With the posters, extra photos of Tina, and some with staple guns in hand, the girls were equipped with what they needed. And, with each team knowing their assigned area, they disbursed.

Casey's mom drove Casey and Janie to their distribution areas of the town and surrounding areas.

Once their job was done, each of the girls went on their separate ways.

Casey's mother dropped Janie off at her house and drove home. She hugged her daughter, "I'm very pleased with you Casey; you initiated the effort to get the word out about your friend."

"And you know, Mom," Casey said, "I spoke with Mr. Lang, my math teacher, while we were out. He says the high school counselor is setting up meetings for students in case we need to talk."

"Oh honey," her mother responded while she cupped Casey's face in her hands, "That's such a good, positive action during this unsettling (and quite upsetting) time for Tina's friends, not knowing what's happened with her. Did you know that the local churches have opened their doors for Tina's family and for the community? They hope to provide peace and comfort, knowing this is such a stressful period."

Casey nodded, "I'm just glad to feel like we're finally doing something in all this."

She and her mother hugged. "I love you, Mom."

"I love you too, my sweet daughter." Her mother kissed Casey's forehead. "I'm thankful you're safe and at home with me now."

Jake called Janie that night, and both were greatly saddened by the official news about Tina's disappearance. Not only were they concerned for Tina, but also they were discouraged at how this could affect their relationship. They had hoped she would show up soon, so she could be the first to know how they feel. But now it appeared she may be gone for a long time. Under the circumstances, they unhappily agreed they should continue to hide how they feel about each other.

"This is so unfair," Jake murmured.

Janie tried to cheer him, "We need to be patient. This is just a temporary thing, anyway. Whatever Tina's going through, it's probably worse than our having to wait for her."

"I know. I just want to spend time with you now, beyond just talking on the cell."

He paused, realizing it was not all about him under the circumstances. He didn't want Janie to view him as selfish. "You're right Janie. We'll be fine."

They were interrupted when Jake's mother wanted him to help her carry the laundry basket of folded clothes upstairs.

"Talk with you tomorrow, my sweetheart," Jake said, and then he began making kissing sounds into the cell.

"Yes, my honey-bunch," Janie responded, also making kissing sounds.

After Jake had hung up, Janie breathed out softly what was in her heart, "Love you."

Chapter 4

During the following weeks, the police continued to actively investigate. They could be seen at the school speaking with students and teachers, their patrol cars were often parked at various neighbor's houses, and they visited with citizens at several of the town's businesses. There was always mention about Tina's disappearance on the radio and television, and in the local newspaper.

One Sunday evening, Casey overheard her parents discussing the situation.

"Honey," her father was saying to her mother, "so far I don't think the police know whether her disappearance was result of a crime or if she simply ran away."

"I know, but they're certainly investigating several of Tina's neighbors and fellow students," her mother responded. "Surely they'll soon find something useful."

Her father poured each of them another cup of hot coffee. "Yeah, well, I heard that Tina's boyfriend, Jake, is now a person of interest."

"Oh my! I can hardly believe he could be involved," her mother said. "Although, remember Mr. Curtis did see those two together just before she disappeared, and they were arguing. She was crying."

"That may or may not mean anything," her dad said.

Casey leaned against the wall she'd been listening from. Mostly concerned with how hurt Janie would be, she moaned, *Oh Lord, please don't let Jake have anything to do with this.*

On Monday, Janie told Casey, "Well, I just heard it, again. Rumor has it that Jake admitted to arguing with Tina on the evening she disappeared, AND he has no solid alibi for the rest of the evening."

Casey adjusted her books in her arms, "Yeah, I also heard that Jake said he went home and watched a movie. But his parents weren't home until late that night. Apparently, nobody saw him go home and the only call he had was when Tina's mom called real late that night."

Janie frowned and bit her lip, "Right. Tina had gone past her curfew without calling her mom." She paused, "Jake is so screwed!" She smacked her locker.

Casey remembered what her dad had said. "Janie, it may not mean anything. We just have to wait and see. I'm just afraid someone snatched her while she was alone."

"Yeah," Janie responded, "Jake didn't do anything. So that's my biggest worry, someone Else...someone mean and awful.. .."

Both of the girls stood quiet, trying not to think of the many possible dark events Tina may be facing.

"But," Casey carefully noted, "I'm just thinking of many possibilities. What if Jake got carried away while they argued?" She paused. "I mean, he may've hurt her accidentally."

Janie shook her head adamantly. "No! That did NOT happen! Jake is so sweet, he'd never hurt anyone. He doesn't even get mad enough to get carried away."

Casey realized her friend could not be objective, not while Jake continued to hold a tender place in her heart. Casey wondered, *maybe they have something going on now?*

Casey placed her hand on Janie's shoulder. "Okay. I'm sorry." They dropped the topic.

During the evening at dinner, Casey's family discussed Tina's disappearance.

"As you might expect," Casey's dad said, "with the $1,000 reward out, the rate of frivolous reports surrounding Tina's whereabouts has increased. And surely, filled with uncertainty and worry, parents would prefer their teens go out in groups rather than to walk or ride bikes solo. I know I do." Dad offered a sideways glance at Casey.

Casey thought, *yeah, and that really sucks for us!*

Mark added, "Yeah. I understand that several girls have complained to the school counselor about having nightmares or anxiety attacks. And us guys have not been doing very well at persuading girls to hang out with us or to even ride in our cars."

So it affects the guys being able to have fun, too. Casey thought. *Good to know!*

Casey's mother observed, "Maybe it's a positive thing, but I believe local parents have become more liberal in grounding their teens."

"I heard a rumor that Tina's body was in the Candice Bay pond, so volunteer divers had to check every inch of it," Casey added.

Casey's dad leaned in, "True, but nothing was found, other than an old tire and some rubbish."

The family sat in silence a few minutes while they finished eating their meal.

Casey's dad cleared his throat to get the others' attention, "No matter how bad the news may be right now, as a normal cycle in humanity's desire and nature's quest to thrive, as time continues, life will seem to move on for neighbors and students here in Candice Bay."

Casey pondered about how much bike riding and walking to town that she could've been doing if it hadn't been for Tina's disappearance. *Well, I can hardly wait till we move on. I feel like I'm being grounded!* But despite how unfair it may feel to her, Casey understood the reasoning behind the actions of the parents in Candice Bay, not just her own. They were making efforts to be careful.

Early one evening, Janie came over to Casey's house to study. Janie's cell phone rang. Once she had answered the call, her face paled. "Who is this? Please stop calling me!" She hung up.

Casey watched her friend fill with fear. *What the heck's going on? Did she get a prank call? Was she threatened? Who would do this to Janie?* Casey asked, "What's this?"

Janie's voice trembled; she was nearly hysterical, "I don't know!"

Casey placed her hand on Janie's shoulder. "No,

really. Who was it? What did they say? I can tell you're VERY upset."

"Yeah, well," Janie said. "I've been getting hang-up calls, and I don't know who it is. They don't say anything and it's starting to creep me out."

"Really? When does it happen?"

"It's always from a private number and always after school, in the evening." Janie paused. "I don't want to tell my parents; it would worry them."

Yeah, always protecting your parents from worry, Casey noted, while concerned for her friend's welfare. Casey believed Janie's parents should try to insulate her from fears and worries, like Casey's parents always do, and not the other way around.

Casey responded, "Yeah, I can understand it creeping you out. You don't say anything to them, do you? I mean, more than you just did? I read an article about that, and any emotion that you show can encourage them, even if you yell at them."

"No, I'm always taken by surprise and don't know what to say. Usually after I say 'hello' a few times, I hang up. But lately I've been more reactive because it's wearing me down."

Almost as a whisper, Janie confided, "I've been having nightmares about it." She shuddered. "Sometimes I don't feel safe, you know?" Tears began to fall down her cheeks.

"I dream that an ugly monster calls me, and after I answer he breaks the door down! He carries me out into a dark, wooded area and I disappear!" She shivered. "There's nothing but blackness after that."

Casey tried to sooth her friend, softly repeating, "It's okay; you're safe now," while she gently hugged her

She shuddered. "I wonder if this happened to Tina before she disappeared, that Tina was abducted by a really awful man, and now he's coming for me!"

"No, that didn't happen to Tina, and it won't happen to you." Casey said this to comfort her friend, but she also worried about the same thing. What if there was a sinister link between Tina's disappearance and Janie now receiving these mysterious calls? Casey fought off her negative thoughts.

Janie cried, "Who would have my cell number to do this anyway?"

Casey reassured her friend. "Really, it's probably just a prank. Anyone can get your cell number if they want it bad enough. It's probably Butch or one of his buddies. Don't let it get to you."

"I know you're right," Janie said, already feeling some relief while she wiped a tear away. She grabbed a tissue to blow her nose.

"Hey, why don't we wrap up our study early and watch a movie? That'll get your mind off all this."

Janie immediately perked up. "Yeah, that sounds great!"

Casey, Janie, and Rusty snuggled on the couch with a big bowl of popcorn and began to watch a good chick-flick. They had decided not to watch anything scary or dramatic, only something happy, peaceful, or comforting. Casey's mom brought them sodas.

While they watched the movie, Janie began thinking about Jake. They'd continued calling each other late at night since Tina's disappearance. These calls had intensified when she began getting prank calls. She knew that Jake wanted to make her feel safe and not have nightmares about the unknown caller. Not having Jake actually with her made her feel vulnerable though. If only the prank calls would stop!

Janie reached for a few pieces of popcorn, as she continued her thoughts about Jake. Because of the circumstances, they had agreed they must keep their relationship a secret. But now he's actually her boyfriend, and she should be able to tell others about this, especially Casey, since she's her best friend.

Janie looked at Casey, wanting to share this secret with her, but she couldn't decide if this was the right time. Casey would surely understand about it whenever she did tell. So what's the big deal? Just spit it out now?

"Um, Casey?"

"Yeah?" Casey asked, still looking at the television.

Quickly, Janie decided not to share about Jake just yet.

Instead, she said, "Could I come over most evenings, for a while, that is?"

"Sure Janie," Casey responded. "I'm sure my folks would be glad to have you here. And I don't think your folks would mind either."

Casey glanced at her friend, *She seems so sad. Maybe this will perk her up!* "Hey, I've got an idea. Come over tomorrow with your college pamphlets and information, and I'll gather mine, too. We can spend the evening making college and med school plans (or dreams)."

Janie smiled. "Oh, that's a great idea!" Janie was delighted that she and her friend share the same career aspirations.

"You know, Janie, we don't have to plan to be nurses."

"Oh, I know," Janie responded, "you can be a doctor, and I might become an echo-cardiologist!" They laughed.

Casey commented, "So true! There are so many specialized areas to choose from within the medical field, like even nuclear medicine."

"Now that sounds important!"

Janie paused, remembering what she'd learned in church to do whenever she had concerns. "Casey, 'something we ought to do." She looked at Casey seriously, "Let's send up special little prayers for Tina whenever we think about her."

Casey nodded her head in agreement. "That's a great idea."

"Remember what our pastor said," Janie reminded Casey, "when two or more pray together, God is right there with us."

"That's a fact," Casey said. "Could you lead us in our prayer tonight?" They prayed for Tina and her family.

I know He'll answer our prayers, Casey told herself. *We just need to be patient.*

Chapter 5

*D*amn! Casey muttered, *I can't wait till I have a car of my own! Now that Mark and Joey have their precious girlfriends, they've dumped me!* Casey found her seat on the bus next to Janie for the short trip to school.

While Casey was busy feeling sorry for herself, Janie chattered about the school's band. Casey decided to quit obsessing about not getting to ride in Mark's Mustang, and she began to listen.

"Anyway, you know the annual drive has started. It's for a good cause—next year's uniforms. Band members have already begun selling candy for this. And, I've volunteered to sell candy to help, too." Janie paused and looked directly into Casey's eyes.

"Casey, I want you to help me with this project." Casey just looked at her.

Janie continued, "Well, are you gonna help me sell candy or not?"

Casey clarified this to herself: Janie's not in the band and doesn't even play an instrument, but she volunteered to sell candy. Janie is always offering to help somebody with something. It's actually rather annoying to watch sometimes, how nice she is. Folks could take advantage of her sweet, sometimes gullible friend.

Casey was confused about Janie's motives. Did she volunteer to help others because she was a loving and kind person or because she wanted to buy the friendships of others? *That's it. She wants to belong! Surely, Janie must know that many people care about her!* Casey would need to talk with her about this sometime.

Then Casey suddenly realized where the interest was: Jake plays the clarinet in the band. *Oh yeah, now I get it! Man, I was really slow this time. I need to pay attention better!*

"Um. Janie?"

Casey had an inquisitive expression on her face, catching Janie's attention and curiosity. "Yeah?"

"Isn't Jake in the band? I mean, he plays the clarinet, right?"

Janie's face turned slightly red and she looked away for a second. "So?"

Casey continued, "So I gather that you and Jake may have something going on. Am I right?"

"Maybe. Maybe not," Janie replied. "You ask too many questions, my friend!"

Casey lightly punched Janie's shoulder, "Okay, I'll stop. For now."

Janie looked at Casey for a few moments. "So I'm still waiting for your answer."

Helping get candy sales for the band was a favor Casey didn't want to be asked to do, so she was tempted to be short. That is, until Casey looked into her sweet friend's big baby-blue eyes. Janie's innocent, sweet expressive eyes melted her resistance, not so different from when Rusty was begging for something, always getting his way, too. As usual, her heart gave in for her friend.

"Yeah, sure, I'll help. We can start by going 'round the neighbors tonight if you want. If our parents will let us."

Casey wondered, *what's the diff? She helps them; I help her.*

Janie laughed with happiness, and with a big smile she shared that she had already gotten a good start.

"Oh, yeah? How's that?"

She explained. While her parents were in the yard talking with Mr. Curtis the previous evening, they mentioned that Janie had volunteered to sell the candy. Mr. Curtis promised to buy a whole case of boxes. What in the world he would be doing with twelve boxes of candy was something she couldn't figure out, unless he planned to donate them to a church or something.

Casey knew Janie liked Mr. Curtis, and he was consistently available to assist Janie. Casey conceded that Mr. Curtis might be genuinely nice, not much different from Janie in temperament. Still, Casey liked to stick with her first impressions because her instincts had always worked well for her. But she admitted, maybe she had no reason to justify a dislike toward this old man. Casey reconsidered her childhood experience. *I don't really know what that was all about. Anyway, they can't all be jerks just because they're old. After all, Dad will be an old man someday, too.*

"Well, maybe my mom will buy some, too. Probably

only one box, though," she said. Then Casey thought she heard the guys behind them laughing, saying something about, "like to buy a *box* from Janie," but she ignored them.

Often the girls heard rude remarks like that when Butch was with the guys. He was their leader, yet just a dumb douchebag as far as Casey was concerned. The boys continued to make suggestive comments and laugh.

Genuinely pissed, Casey glanced at Janie to see if she too heard them, but whether she did or not, she seemed ignorant and remained cheery. That made Casey more upset with the guys *and* with Janie. *Catch a clue, girl!*

Once they'd made it to their lockers, Casey quickly surveyed the contents of hers. Yep, another note *and* a red silk rose, too. *A new mystery! How did the silk rose get into my locker? Or was this really so unusual? How many friends did I share my combination with? Geez, I may never get to the bottom of this!*

Casey quickly stuffed her rose into her gym bag (where she kept her notes hidden) and covered it with her towel. Lately the letters were becoming a little strange. Sometimes the admirer expressed disappointment that Casey didn't react. She would've gone to the school's administration, but school would soon be out for the summer. Maybe then all of this would stop without her having to do anything.

Sometimes she worried it might even be Butch doing this, and she didn't know how she'd be able to handle that. She carefully looked around, figuring an admirer would watch her discover these gifts, but the only guys regularly around her locker were Butch and his buddies. Ugh!

Casey would be in the midst of daydreaming about Steve revealing himself to her, imagining they had a romance blooming, even the two of them in some hot scenes (like hanging out at his car), then she'd see Butch standing at her locker and her mental pictures of Steve would be ruined.

Casey and Janie had barely gotten their books situated when Butch came along and threw his arm over Janie's shoulder. "Hey little cutie, I want to buy some *candy*, some of *your* delicious *boxes* of candy." And he began to laugh suggestively.

He even ran his hand along his groin area. Casey said, "Disgusting!" His followers watched nearby. They too made vulgar gestures.

Butch began touching Janie's face and arms. Like in a bad movie, he said, "Hey, baby, now don't get mad. You know you like it."

When Janie tried to move away from Butch, he quickly pinned her to the locker. He was clearly enjoying holding a pretty girl captive, even if it was for only a moment.

Casey pulled her face close to Butch and yelled at him right in his ear, "GO away! Go away NOW!" but he ignored her, moving his body closer against Janie. It was as if he'd zoned out for a few seconds.

Just then, Mark came walking by. He placed his hand heavily on Butch's shoulder. "Now, Butch, my man, is this any way to treat a pretty young lady?" He slowly began squeezing his hand tightly. Butch bristled, regretting that he hadn't checked the hall before pouncing on Janie.

Mark often lifted weights with Joey, and he was a key player on the wrestling team. Butch knew he would be no match in any fight with Mark.

Not wanting to risk having a humiliating fight with Mark in front of fellow students and especially in front of his followers, Butch mumbled something not quite audible and stepped away. Just as quickly, he composed himself and said, "Hey! I musta got my signals crossed. I thought Janie *wanted* my attention."

"No, Butch, I don't ever want you touching me," Janie clearly responded. Then she gave Casey a big grin, knowing that she'd just been braver than she had ever been. It felt good to her, really good.

Casey cheered, "Big whoop, whoop!" Then Casey added, "Oh, and in case you didn't know it, Butch, I don't want anything to do with you either! Dickhead!"

Smiling, Mark stood by the girls. As Casey watched Butch saunter down the hall, she decided that even though it was only a few weeks before school ended, she would ask the school's administration to change her locker (and Janie's) so they wouldn't be in the same proximity as Butch any longer. That could solve her situation with her admirer, too, because he most likely would not find her new locker's location. She would not be sharing her combination again.

Casey fussed at herself for not thinking of this simple solution earlier.

That night after her parents had gone to bed, Janie quietly slipped out onto her porch to meet Jake, who was sitting in her porch swing. After spending many nights talking on the phone until morning, they decided it was all right for them to see each other at her house when nobody would know. Besides, not knowing when or if Tina may return, their patience had completely run out.

Their hearts beating with excitement, they sat close, holding hands. This went on for quite some time, just quietly sitting together, happy to be together at last. They began to whisper and look deep into each other's eyes.

"Janie, I can hardly wait until this whole Tina mess is out of the way. I want everyone to know you're my girl." He paused. "I just wish she'd come back or we'd find out what happened with her."

"I know. It's the not knowing that's hard. And not being able to tell everyone that you're my boyfriend." Janie suddenly felt shy after calling him her boyfriend with them now face-to-face. She focused her attention to their entwined hands.

Jake smiled and cupped her face into his hands. He affectionately kissed her cheek and then sprinkled kisses on her lips. Janie responded by hugging him closer to her, and returning light kisses to him. He ran his fingers through her silky hair while they continued to kiss.

A cat screeched after a trash can tumbled by the roadside, breaking the night's silence. Jake and Janie realized that he should leave. They hugged and kissed

their good-byes, and he watched while she slipped back in to the house.

Jake regretted that their first visit had been cut so short, but he then assured himself that this was merely their beginning. They will have a lifetime together.

Chapter 6

"What! You must be kidding!" said the school's assistant principal, Mrs. London.

"Yes," Casey explained, "Butch and his friends have been bothering Janie and me almost constantly this school term. I'm sorry I didn't bring it to your attention until now."

"Well, I'm particularly upset that Butch held Janie against her locker. We have zero tolerance in this school for such physically aggressive behavior," said Mrs. London. "I assure you, Casey, I will make issue about this with all parents involved—Butch's, Janie's, and yours. And since he's already received at least one other warning, I can assure you that regardless of whether any formal charges are made, Butch will leave you two alone while at school from now on."

Casey regretted telling Mrs. London before having shared her story with her parents. This would not go down well with her mom. "Um, is it really necessary to get my parents involved?"

Mrs. London nodded. "Honey, he crossed the line. This is a very serious matter, and our school administration must respond accordingly."

Oh no! Now I really wish I'd said something to Mom. Janie had better tell her parents, too, right away! Casey swallowed hard, knowing her parents would have to be told about the next issue as well.

"Well, Mrs. London, I have something else I should tell you," Casey said.

Mrs. London looked up from the information she had on her tablet. "Yes?"

"Well," Casey began, "for a few months now, I've been getting notes from someone. They were left in my locker and not signed."

Mrs. London cocked her head and wrinkled her brow. "Notes? What do your notes say? Do they contain anything threatening or sexual in nature?"

"Oh no, not that far out. They're just romantic. Sometimes the notes have drawings, like hearts. One time a poem that had been copied from a book was included in the note. Other times, maybe the poems were made up." Casey paused to reflect.

"Lately, there's been a silk red rose included sometimes. I don't know how they got my combination number. The notes seemed to become more needy and sad. The person talked about being disappointed in me."

Mrs. London leaned back in her chair and asked, "How so? Can you explain it to me?"

"Geez, I don't know. I don't even know who it is, so I can't figure out what they expect of me. And I don't understand the roses. I have three of them, so far."

"Here, I kept it all in this." Casey handed Mrs. London

her gym bag filled with all of the notes and roses.

Mrs. London silently examined each item while Casey waited. Mrs. London was very interested and seemed to know who might be doing this. She asked many questions. Then she said something that Casey found unusual.

"Do you know Marla? Marla Sims?" Casey looked at her for a few minutes. *Why in the world would you ask me that? Has this happened to her?*

"Well, yeah, she's in a couple of my classes. Has somebody been doing this to her, too?"

Mrs. London hesitated. "Not exactly, but I'll check this out. We're going to have to talk with your mother about this as well. Does she know?" She added information to her tablet. The silence answered her question.

Mrs. London looked straight through Casey. "Please tell your parents about this right away. I'll be making some phone calls and doing some checking first, and then I must meet with your parents, this evening if possible. In the meantime, Casey, it's imperative that you do not share this information with anyone else, other than your parents, of course."

She waited, but Casey didn't respond. "Do you understand me?" Mrs. London said.

And Janie, of course, Casey told herself.

Casey nodded, "Yes, Mrs. London." She shuffled her feet on the floor. "Can I go now?" and Mrs. London motioned for her to wait a moment while the assistant principal pulled out a business card from her desk drawer. "I want you to have my card with my cell phone number." She held it out.

"Here, so you and your parents can call me with any questions or to discuss these matters with me. And call immediately if you need me."

Casey took her card and stashed it into the front pocket of her jeans.

She rushed out of the room, anxious that Mrs. London might contact her mother before she had shared the information first.

Casey could hardly keep up with other students' conversations while she waited for the bus. She worked the story in her mind, rehearsing what she would say to her mother. Janie kept on talking, as if she was unaware that Casey wasn't listening; she wasn't interested in the progress of band candy sales anyway.

"Janie, please shut up!" Casey said. Janie stopped instantly, knowing something was terribly wrong. Casey never spoke to her like that.

"Janie, I told Mrs. London everything about Butch and his friends bullying us. So you've gotta tell your parents right away, 'cause she'll be contacting them tonight." Casey paused. "I'm really sorry that I didn't tell you before now."

Janie's face fell and her eyes widened. "That's alright. It needed to come out sometime. I've been thinking about telling my parents anyway. I'll tell them right after I get off the bus."

Whew, what a relief, Casey thought. *Thank you, Janie, for understanding.*

Finally Casey arrived home. She had hoped Mark would soon be home so he would support her while she shared her story, but Mark had gone to the store for car parts.

Only Casey's mother was there because her dad was working out of town for the next couple of days. Casey lay on her bed, staring at the ceiling. She tried to take her mind off the conversation she needed to have with her mom by listening to some music, but her mind could not travel far. She feared the phone would ring before she had a chance to talk to her mom, but she also feared having the conversation without Mark beside her.

Casey continued to wait for Mark to return, but he was late for dinner. Finally she decided, *Okay, now's the time to tell. He's not showing up.*

Her mom led the dinner blessing, and before food was served, Casey began her dreaded tale.

"Oh, um, Mom. There's some things I need to tell you about that's been going on at school."

Her mother stopped serving the peas. "Are you in trouble?" she said. She sat down, ready to listen.

"No, nothing like that." Casey bit her lip. "Well, for one thing, Butch and his friends have been annoying Janie and me, like they always do, but today he pushed Janie against the locker."

"Oh, my! Casey, did he hurt her?"

"No, maybe he would've, but Mark showed up and pretty much ran Butch off." Casey began with Butch's most recent and most violent act. She didn't think her mother would have taken her seriously if she'd just mentioned about his bothering them. Her mom would probably think the girls were being too sensitive.

Now that Casey had gotten her mother's attention with the inappropriate touching, her mother patiently listened to the rest of the story.

"Well," her mother said, "I'm going to thank that wonderful son of mine for rescuing the two of you today, and this bullying has to come to a stop right now."

Her mother shared that Janie's parents would probably press charges once they knew.

Oh geez! This is so hard! Casey thought to herself. *Why did I hold it all back?*

"Yeah." Casey continued, "that's not the only thing." She hesitated, not sure how to present the rest of her story.

"Okay now, spit it all out, young lady and we'll deal with it." Her mother crossed her arms in front of her chest.

"Well, I think I have a secret admirer," Casey said.

Her mother started to smile, but noticed it was not a fun event for her daughter. "Oh? Please go on."

Casey said, "Somebody's been leaving me love notes in my locker. Not just notes though, poems and drawings and even some silk roses."

"Really now. Do you have any idea who may be doing this?"

"No," Casey said. "But I've been trying to figure it out."

Mark walked into the dining area in time to hear the end of the conversation. He asked, "What are you talking about? Is it Butch?"

Immediately, his mother jumped up and gave him a

big hug. "Oh yes, dear, we were talking about Butch. I am so proud of you for helping your little sister and her friend today. You saved them from that big bully." She planted a kiss on each of his cheeks and motioned for him to sit at the table. She began serving his plate.

Mark said, "Yeah, it looked like he had gone a bit too far. He was pressed up against Janie, and it sure didn't look like he planned to stop, not on his own anyway."

Mark looked seriously at Casey, "I think the incident should be reported, sis."

"I agree, and I did," Casey replied.

"You did?" their mother asked. "When did you report it?"

"Yep, I did it right before school let out, and I told about that other thing, too."

"What other thing?" Mark asked.

Their mother instructed, "Casey, please explain to Mark what you know about your secret admirer."

Casey shared the details and ended by letting them know that Mrs. London had all of the notes, poems, drawings, and silk red roses and would probably be calling tonight.

"I had assumed my precious daughter was safe at school every day. I question how much I really know about you, my beautiful teenage girl. You're also my baby." She smiled and patted Casey's hand. "But, it probably shouldn't be such a surprise. Teenage girls are known to be somewhat secretive."

"Mom. So you do understand?" Casey asked, "And you forgive me?"

Casey's mom quickly nodded. "Yes my dear. Of course I do."

Mark said, "You know, Casey, these unsolicited gifts could be normal overtures for a teenage romance. Or not!"

Their mother interjected, "Or he might be a stalker!"

Once the meal was finished, their mother announced, "I'm contacting Mrs. London right now."

Casey gave her the business card from Mrs. London and began to clear the dishes.

"Hello, Mrs. London? This is Belinda Trent, Casey's mother. How are you today?"

"Yes, Belinda. Hi, I'm glad to get to speak with you. It's been a while, hasn't it?" She continued, "Please call me Jennifer."

"Well, yes, Jennifer, it has been a while. I meant to meet with you last month to go over Casey's career planning, but my schedule just didn't allow for it."

"Oh my, I certainly do understand that," Mrs. London said. "My schedule is usually kept quite busy, too." She paused. "So hey, Belinda, I'm so glad that you called because I was just about to contact you. Have you had time to speak with Casey this evening?"

"Yes," Belinda said. "My daughter has been telling me some disturbing stories."

"I'm so sorry to be dealing with such unpleasant matters," Jennifer said.

"Mrs. London, I mean Jennifer, I'm quite upset about these situations she's been telling me about. What do you know about them? And what is the school going to do?"

Jennifer hesitated, "I can appreciate your concern. Right after Casey and I spoke today, I did some checking around, and I believe I can now share with you what is going on."

"Okay."

Mrs. London continued, "I'm in town right now, not far from Candice Bay. Would it be possible for me to stop by for a few minutes tonight?"

Belinda quickly responded, "Yes, but can you share with me now any resolution you may have come up with at this point? Please tell me."

"Belinda, I'd really like to go over it in more depth with you in person, but I can say that the school is already handling both matters and I feel certain that our approach will meet your satisfaction."

"Okay. Thank you, and I appreciate your stopping by tonight."

Mrs. London arrived within the hour. Mark vacated the house before this important meeting began.

Belinda and Mrs. London sat on the living room sofa sipping coffee, while Casey and Rusty sat in the adjoining chair feeling like they were the guilty ones. The secret admirer items covered the coffee table.

"As for the problems with Butch, we are taking immediate steps to remedy this problem," she said. "After I checked with various staff and employees, a witness did come forward. Our janitor, William, reported that he saw the entire incident, and his story collaborates with your daughter's.

I assure you that Butch will no longer be bothering the girls while at school. We have a zero tolerance for such actions, and I doubt he will be welcome at our school any longer. Janie's parents will have to decide if they wish to pursue this matter legally."

She changed from her rigid stature to a more relaxed posture. "As for the unsolicited locker gifts, I've been given permission to speak on this. I think I can shed some light as to whom the admirer is and the potential motives."

Casey and Rusty leaned in with great interest. *All right! I can finally learn who my secret admirer may be. I'm so excited!*

Mrs. London cleared her throat. "We've been aware of some problems with a student at our school for some time now, and we've been keeping very careful track of her. She is not considered to be dangerous to anyone."

Casey interrupted, "Huh? You do know it was a *guy* doing this, not a girl, right?"

Mrs. London looked into Casey's face. "I'm sorry Casey, but we're talking about Marla Sims. She has some personal problems, but it appears she's really only a danger to herself. Do you have any idea what I might be talking about?" The assistant principal waited for this information to sink in. "Do you know much about Marla?"

Casey tried to understand. *What the heck does this have to do with my situation? Marla was my admirer? What? There goes my Steve out of my life before we had a chance!*

Casey responded, "She's always quiet and by herself. She's either a cutter or a druggie, because she always wears long sleeved tops, even when it's hot weather. Some of the girls make fun of her. They call her 'Cutter' and 'Emo.' They say it close enough for her to hear them, too. But I try to be nice to her. She seems sad."

Mrs. London looked toward Belinda and said, "Marla's father gave me permission to speak on this. Regardless, I'm not at liberty to disclose personal psychological information about one student to another student's family."

Belinda interrupted, "I only want to know this: Is she a danger to Casey? I mean, is she unstable? Why would she be sending my daughter love letters and flowers?"

"I can't be sure since I'm not a psychiatrist, but it appears that she might have developed some emotional issues. More than likely, if Casey had not told me about these incidents before school let out for the summer, Marla would have become more emotional and depressed from what she might see as Casey's rejection."

"Why would she think I'd be interested?" Casey said with shock and disgust. "Just because I don't have a boyfriend doesn't mean I'm GAY!" *Oh, this is totally disgusting!* She became more boisterous. "No, I'm straight! I didn't do *anything* to make her think I had any interest that way."

Casey wasn't sure how she should feel: mad, insulted, or just sorry for poor Marla. *So much for my daydream of ANY handsome guy!* She was feeling a jumble of emotions.

"I'm sure there was nothing on your part to encourage her at all," Mrs. London gently said. "What she seems to want is to have someone to confide in about her cutting." Mrs. London reached her hand out to Casey, showing her understanding. "You have probably been nicer to her than most of the girls, so she felt maybe she could approach you."

She sat back and studied her audience to get an idea of their reactions. "Belinda, this much I can share because it became public knowledge within our school system and the area. Marla and her father left Hanover County three years ago and moved to Candice Bay. Her mother had been arrested for abusing Marla and lost custody of her. It was in the news and indirectly revealed information that Marla might be a cutter."

Mrs. London paused. "Please know that was three years ago. Marla has probably continued cutting. No doubt, social services ended Marla and her mother's visits following her arrest. Such childhood trauma and emotional pain may have contributed to her current issues."

Mrs. London leaned forward in her seat. "I assure you now that the school, her father, and her psychiatrist don't believe she's suicidal or a danger to anyone else. Marla seems to be a sad little girl going through a difficult teenage transitional period and trying to find ways to cope with her ongoing inner pain."

Belinda leaned forward in her seat. "Jennifer, as a mother, my first concern has to be for my daughter. Even if Marla is not a danger to her, she can't continue sending love notes, either." She pointed at Casey, "You've heard her speak out about it, and obviously this does bother her."

With admiration toward her mother, Casey thought, *that's right mom. Stand up for me!*

"Belinda, Casey, I assure you that Marla will not be bothering Casey any further. And, there's no reason for anyone else to have knowledge of the locker gifts."

Relieved, Casey said, "Thank you, Mrs. London. I would die if anyone knew!" Casey silently prayed, *and thank you, Lord!*

Belinda said, "Yes, I too appreciate this."

Some moments of silence passed.

"Jennifer, that is just awful about Marla," Belinda said, "and I'm sure it's very hard for her and her father. What's going to become of her? Can she be cured?"

"I don't know what will become of her," Mrs. London said. "Whatever help she is getting, the progress appears to be in tiny, baby steps. She admitted to the notes, but denies the flowers. She's apparently mixed up right now."

She turned to Casey and said, "I don't believe she will be able to come to school in the fall. I'm so sorry that you and your family had to be pulled into this sad mess."

Belinda said, "What can we do to help?"

"I hope," directing her attention again to Casey, "that you will be able to find it within yourself to be kind and understanding whenever, or if, the two of you cross paths in the future."

Casey nodded. "Yeah. I've been nice to her anyway, and I haven't been talking about her or making fun of her either."

"I know. Like I said earlier, that's probably why she tried to reach out to you. Now that the situation is known, she is working this out with her psychiatrist's and father's help."

"Again, let me say, you don't need to worry about her bothering you any further," Mrs. London said. "But if she or anyone else does anything strange or unusual like this in the future, I want you to tell me immediately, alright?"

Belinda broke in, "Oh yes! And your MOTHER should be told about it first!"

Casey agreed, thinking, *oh yes, I've learned my lesson.*

"Before you leave, Jennifer, I wonder if you could talk with me for a moment about the high school's graduating class. Are we still going to have the graduation ceremony like every year? I mean, in light of how the students feel about Tina being missing?" She added, "I'm asking because my son, Mark, graduates this year and I don't see any plans happening."

Mrs. London seemed deep in thought. "You know, I'm not sure. We had a meeting about it and could not arrive at an agreement. Some wanted to put the ceremony off until July even though we've completed preparation for it. I think that we're leaning toward a very short and quick ceremony with perhaps a small mention about Tina and her family being in our thoughts."

Belinda explained, "I wondered because Tina's disappearance has definitely placed a damper on these students wanting to celebrate anything at this juncture. But, they certainly have a right to a graduation ceremony, as did the classes in other years."

Jennifer asked, "And, what does your son say about it?"

Belinda paused before responding. "At first he said that he and some other friends plan to just get their diplomas in the mail. But I don't know if he really meant that."

This seemed to confirm the school staff's idea. Mrs. London said, "Yes, I think the ceremony will have to be short and sweet this year because our students are on an emotional roller coaster right now."

They both shook their heads and dropped the subject.

After Mrs. London left, Belinda and Casey prayed for Marla, that God would heal her from hurting and cutting and that she would become the happy, healthy young woman she should be. As they had been doing for some time now, they prayed for Tina and her family.

Casey thanked God for her many blessings in life that she all too often took for granted. She was so thankful that she didn't have such hard issues to deal with. She vowed she would strive not to make fun of anyone who appeared different and she'd try to be patient with them, because she had no idea what another person might be going through.

That night, Jake and Janie sat on her front porch steps together with only scant light from a neighbor's front porch lantern that cast silhouettes of the couple.

Irritated with the news about Butch's assault, Jake whispered, "You should've at least told me about it, Janie. I'm your boyfriend, after all."

Janie lowered her head. "I'm sorry. I didn't tell my parents, either. I just wanted the whole thing to disappear like it didn't really happen." She paused. "Anyway, I'm fine now. When Casey called me, she told me Mrs. London told her and Casey's mom that

Butch would *not* be bothering us again. I think they're gonna expel him."

"Yeah, but it could've turned out much differently, especially with Butch not knowing that you have a boyfriend who would do anything to protect you."

Janie's eyes watered up. "Jake, I said I was sorry. If only we didn't have to hide our relationship from the world, he probably wouldn't have even approached me."

Jake remained disturbed that he was helpless in preventing Butch from attacking his girl, but he also didn't want to cause Janie any further upset than she had already endured.

He gently placed his hand at her chin, gave her a brief kiss on the cheek, and said, "I'm sorry, and I understand." He hugged her, "Actually, I'm glad the school administration knows, and Butch won't be able to bother you anymore."

He looked in to Janie's eyes, "Soon, everyone will know that you're my girl. And there won't be incidents like this to be bothered with."

Janie smiled, "You're right, Jake. And I can hardly wait."

They sat quietly, holding each other.

Janie raised up, "Jake, Casey also told me tonight that someone's been putting notes and flowers in her locker for some time now."

"Really? How long has this been going on?" Jake mused, "And I wonder who it is?"

"I don't know how long. I guess we're not the only ones keeping secrets." She smiled at Jake. "Anyway,

Mrs. London thinks it was Marla doing it. She seemed sure of it."

Jake placed his hand on his chin and his brows lowered, "Marla the cutter? That doesn't sound right. Why would Mrs. London blame her?"

"Apparently Casey's been kind to Marla. You know, in the midst of many making fun of her." Janie scratched her forehead. "So with Marla being a loner and so mixed up anyway, I guess she became desperate for Casey to be her friend."

"Well. I guess that could make sense. Marla's a real mess. I feel sorry for her too."

Janie frowned, "Yeah. Lots of us felt sorry for her, but we didn't say anything. Marla probably thought then that everyone was against her."

Jake added, "And then there was Casey. Knowing her, she probably took up for Marla a few times."

Janie smiled, "Yeah. She's not afraid to say what she thinks, that's for sure. I wish I could be more like that."

Jake hugged Janie, "You're perfect, just the way you are." He peppered kisses on her cheeks.

Janie giggled, and started to say something, but then they heard someone walking around the living room from inside the house.

Startled, Janie whispered, "I think that's my dad. He might open the door any minute!"

They both stood up, with hands clasped. Jake lowered his head to her face, "Yeah. Gotta go, sweetie," giving Janie a quick kiss on the lips.

Janie watched him walk to the street. He turned briefly, and she blew kisses at him. He waved and rushed out of sight.

Janie quietly opened the door, peeked around, and stepped in. She gently closed the door. At that moment her dad came into the living room from the kitchen, with a sandwich in one hand, and a glass of water in the other.

"Janie dear. Did I wake you?"

"No Dad, I just thought I'd get a glass of water."

Her dad smiled at her, "Okay then. Good night."

She hugged his waist as he passed by her, "Good night, Dad."

Chapter 7

The next school day, Casey and the other girls in P.E. finished their soccer game and left the gym. They headed for the locker room to shower and change their clothes. Tish, one of the black girls in her class, had accidently bumped Marcia. Marcia was one of the rich, white, snobby girls. Tish immediately said, "Oh, excuse me!"

But Marcia would not let it go. "That's right. You'd better say excuse me and get your black ass outta my way!" Three of Marcia's friends moved near Marcia to show support. Tish was not the type to back down from any challenge. Her larger group of supporters began closing in on the incident.

Marcia gave Tish a shove, and that was it. Tish came out slugging, as did her friends, and they were getting the better of these snobs who had resorted to pulling hair and kicking.

Oh my God! Casey yelled, "Stop this!" She instructed another girl, Tonya, to get some help and Tonya ran out to get the teacher. Tonya looked more than happy to have a reason to get out of the room. This was a really bad place for a fight to break out, with too much privacy in the locker room from the teachers' intervention and hard fixtures that could hurt a person.

Tish kept whaling on Marcia, slugging her in the face and stomach. Marcia was dazed and fell to the floor for the last time. While Marcia lay there, Tish kicked her in the ribs and prepared to give a serious power kick to her head, saying, "DIE, bitch!"

But Casey, seeing what Tish was about to do, gave her a hard shove, causing Tish to lose her balance.

At that moment, the P.E. instructor and two other teachers rushed into the room, "Break it up! Break it up now! Anyone who continues gets automatic suspension!"

Tish glared at Casey, "You shoulda minded your own business." She leaned in to Casey so no one else could hear her, "I'm gonna break you in half, bitch!"

Casey stared at her, as if unafraid, but she was terrified by the hatred in Tish's eyes.

Mrs. London soon came to the scene and instructed the P.E. teacher, "Becka, I want the names of everyone in this class, and you are to identify who was in Marcia's group and those who were in Tish's group."

"Yes, Mrs. London," said Mrs. Green, and she rushed to her office to gather the requested information.

Another teacher announced, "Ambulances and the police department have been called. We're keeping the injured girls stable until the ambulances arrive."

Mrs. London nodded, "Thank you. What are the injuries?"

The teacher responded, "It appears Marcia's face is

a mess and probably she has one or more fractured ribs. Another girl has a long laceration down her arm, probably requiring stitches. All of the others have minor cuts and bruises."

The police officers arrived first. Mrs. London greeted the officer in charge and assured him that the police department would have everyone's complete cooperation while they investigated this situation. Sergeant Wade agreed to interview the girls in Mrs. London's office with her present, for everyone's convenience and in hopes to promote a more peaceful, cooperative environment.

Mrs. London instructed a nearby teacher, "Please tell Mrs. Green to have all of the girls report to my office immediately for interviews."

Mrs. Green came back into the girl's locker room where police were collecting evidence. She found a moment alone with Mrs. London and said, "Mrs. London, I know it's too early to think about what disciplinary actions there may be, but I understand that two of the girls in this incident were seniors."

The girls waited in line at Mrs. London's office for their interviews. Rumor had it that those seniors could be deprived of receiving their diplomas for an extended period and they worried that the school administration would actually do that.

Mrs. Green came into the hallway where girls sat in chairs awaiting their turn. She looked at her tablet to read the first name listed. "Sandy?"

"Yes, Mrs. Green." Sandy responded timidly with

her eyes opened wide.

"Come with me."

Sandy got up and slowly followed Mrs. Green into the office where Sergeant Wade and Mrs. London sat at her large conference table.

Mrs. London greeted her, "Sandy. This is Sergeant Wade. He has a few informal questions to ask you. This is only an interview. You are not making a police statement at this time, so your parents are not required to be with us. Do you understand?"

Sandy nervously sat in the chair across from them. "Yes, Mrs London. I understand."

Sergeant Wade cleared his throat and opened his portfolio, and pulled out a pad of paper. With pen in hand he began the interview. "Sandy, were you in the girl's locker room today when the fight broke out?"

"Yes sir."

"Please tell me, in your own words, what happened."

Sandy grasped her hands and looked at them. "Well. I was changing clothes near Marcia, when Tish bumped her. Then words were said back and forth, and then suddenly Tish started hitting Marcia. Me and some other girls tried to help Marcia, and then Tish's friends started hitting on us. It was crazy. I don't remember much after that. I was busy trying not to get hurt."

Sergeant Wade continued to scribble on his pad of paper, then looked up briefly to ask, "So who started the fight, Sandy?"

Sandy shuffled her feet and coughed. "Well, Tish did. We were just changing clothes when she came over, for no reason. She approached us."

Sergeant Wade looked into Sandy's face. "We. Who was with you and Marcia, changing?"

Sandy looked down at her hands. "I don't really remember now. It's all a blur, really."

Sergeant Wade nodded to Mrs. London, and Mrs. London said, "That will be all for now, Sandy. Go back to class, and don't speak about this interview with anyone. Thank you."

Sandy quickly got up, wiped the perspiration from her forehead, and mumbled, "Yes Mrs. London," and she rushed out the door.

The next person called from the list was Jasmine. Her story was in direct conflict with Sandy's story. She believed that Tish stumbled while passing Marcia, so Marcia made a racial slur and Marcia and her group of white girls ganged up on Tish, all at once. Jasmine and a few others only joined in to keep Tish from getting badly hurt.

After Jasmine left the room, Sergeant Wade explained to Mrs. London, "I'm not really surprised at the conflicting stories. What I'm waiting for is a student that wasn't on one of the two sides in this fight to present a more realistic view of what happened. That's where we'll get closer to the truth."

Mrs. London nodded, "Yes, I see. I believe we have a few who were not on either side. They just happened to be too close in proximity, and got caught up into the fighting."

While Casey waited for her turn, she reviewed the incident. It was strange and scary how quickly nice, decent girls could become primitive and hostile with each other, and over such stupid stuff! Maybe it was a racist thing, but Marcia seemed to think she was better than everyone, regardless of race.

Casey muttered, "Marcia started it, being such a snot! Will that girl ever learn?"

Although Tish was known to have her harsh moments, she and Casey had never had any problems. Casey was still surprised at Tish's threatening words. Maybe in time— a lot of time—Tish would be able to see that Casey had actually helped prevent her from seriously ruining her own future.

Casey felt icky having to rat on her classmates, but was truthful during her interview. That is, except for the part where Tish aimed for Marcia's head and her threats. Casey felt a tugging in her heart, as if she were being instructed to be quiet about the bad part. She felt an urging; "Be quiet; let it pass."

Finally it was Casey's turn for the interview. Sergeant Wade had already been interviewing students for an hour, and when Casey walked into the room he was sipping on hot coffee that Mrs. Green had brought in. He asked Casey how the fight started.

Casey sat straight in her seat, with her hands cupped together. She looked at Mrs. London and then at Sergeant Wade. "It looked to me like Tish accidently bumped Marcia, and then apologized. But Marcia smarted off to Tish, and told her to get her black ass outta her way. Then Marcia shoved Tish. That started the fight."

Sergeant Wade asked, while still looking at his pad, "So which group were you friends with, Marcia's or Tish's?"

Casey responded, "I wasn't on either side. I had hoped I was a friend, or at least an acquaintance with both groups."

Sergeant Wade smiled and nudged Mrs. London. She gave him a knowing look.

"So you weren't involved in the fighting at all?" He asked.

Casey wanted to be truthful, yet be very brief about her part. "I sent someone for help and shoved some, just trying to break it up."

Sergeant Wade soon dismissed Casey. He smiled at Mrs. London, once Casey was gone. "Now that, Mrs. London, appears to be one of our neutral girls that I was looking for. We may have more questions for her later on."

After the interview, Casey wondered why she had omitted telling on Tish. Was she afraid of what Tish might do? No. Did she have compassion for her, knowing Tish acted in the heat of the moment, that she was not an evil person? More than anything, Casey wondered if God had been speaking to her. She decided the matter was not for her to figure out. It was up to God to work changes in Tish.

The next morning, Janie called Casey.

"Well Casey, I'm surprised you didn't hear my dad cussing this morning, that the whole Candice Bay didn't hear him."

"What are you talking about, Janie?" Casey asked, "I've never heard your dad cuss."

Janie responded, "He cussed so loud when he discovered that someone took black paint to my bike while it was chained to the porch post. And, they wrote 'Bitch' on the porch floor!"

"Oh my God! I think I'd cuss too if I were your dad!" Casey paused. "This time, Janie, I really do think Butch did it."

Janie agreed, "Yeah, I think it was his retaliation for our tattling about his holding me to the locker." For a moment, Casey wondered if Tish could've done it because Janie was Casey's best friend. *No, it would be her style to come after me directly.*

Janie said, "You know Casey, Mom and Dad are too fearful to tell about this vandalism and they want to let it go rather than report it to the police. Tomorrow, Mom plans to try to clean the paint off, and when she's done, Dad plans to repaint the entire porch. We just want to forget it ever happened."

"Well," Casey said, "I guess you know that in the process, you're essentially covering up any possible evidence by cleaning and painting the porch. So there won't be evidence available to point to who did this."

Frustrated for Janie and with her family's response to the crime, Casey reminded Janie about what they'd learned in school: the proper way to respond to the destruction of property is to get information to the proper authorities. Otherwise, the victim actually supports the criminal or perpetrator and indirectly encourages him to act out again. Most likely the acts of crime would escalate.

Casey wondered, *could any of this bad stuff happening be connected to what happened to Tina?*

Telling Janie what she considered proper handling of this crime only seemed to cause sadness, and Casey regretted talking about it. *Hmmm. What can I do to distract Janie from all this?*

"Janie, how would you like to help me babysit the monster twins on Saturday night?" Casey asked.

"The monster twins? Oh yeah, Joey's little brother and sister." Janie paused. "Maybe."

"I'll give you half of my earnings," Casey said.

Janie nodded her head. "Yeah, sure. I could use some money right now."

The twins are fun kids; they could also be exhausting for a teen to babysit alone. Casey and Janie planned to play heartily with the children. Bret likes to play rough games with his trucks, or run with a ball, while Betsey would be happy to play imaginary dress up or tea party with very few props. Casey and Janie decided that they could switch from one child to the other, to give the kids a variety and to keep them busy.

Chapter 8

"Why is Rusty going with us on this babysitting job?" Janie asked, while she and Casey walked down the sidewalk from Casey's house to Joey's, each wearing a backpack filled with clothing and toiletries needed to spend the night, and Casey leading Rusty along by his leash.

"Because, Bret and Betsy love Rusty and they asked me to bring him next time I came over," Casey explained. "Rusty might help keep the kids entertained."

"I don't know about that Casey," Janie paused. "I seem to remember you telling me a story about catching Bret trying to tie Rusty to a chair so he could feed Rusty like a baby."

"Well, yeah. That did happen, but Rusty didn't get hurt, and he didn't growl or even show his teeth." Casey paused. "I wasn't watching the twins as well as I should. This time you'll be with me. Surely between the two of us, we can make sure they don't hurt Rusty."

"I hope you're right." Janie sighed, "Still, you don't want to push a dog to the limit when with children."

The girls stood in front of Joey's house for a moment and the kids quickly opened the door. Bret and Betsy laughed and smiled as they ran off the porch and down the sidewalk toward Rusty. Meanwhile Rusty wiggled his body and jumped up to greet them.

While the kids were on their knees hugging Rusty, Casey said, "Aren't you going to welcome Janie and me, too?" Bret and Betsy gave Casey and Janie a hug.

"Come on!" Bret said excitedly. "We have a surprise for you!"

They all went into the house to find that Bret and Betsy had made cookies.

"Momma helped us!" Betsy explained with a big grin.

The children's parents gave Casey and Janie scant instructions before leaving. It wasn't long before the children and Rusty had settled down with toys on the living room floor.

Janie and Casey looked out the front window as some bikers rode by. "Oh Janie, do you know the girl with the burgundy pants?" Casey asked. "Melissa?"

"Yes, I know her. She sure does have a mouth on her, doesn't she!" Janie responded.

Casey continued, "Yeah. Well, let me tell you what Sherri told me yesterday."

"Oh, I think I already know." Janie paused. "But tell me what you heard."

As they discussed the latest gossip about Melissa, Casey heard a funny sound coming from the other room. "Wait a sec. Listen, what's that?"

Janie listened too.

It was Rusty gently whining from the other room.

Casey and Janie quickly ran into the dining area in time to see Betsy and Bret trying to put a doll's hat on poor little Rusty, having already fitted him with a doll's dress.

Casey was furious. "Bret! Get away from Rusty! You too, Miss Betsy!" Casey grabbed Rusty and he whimpered. No doubt, he believed Casey was his hero. She held him close.

While Casey carefully undressed Rusty, she shouted at the twins, "You're both in time out!" and she pointed to the nearest corners.

The twins began to cry. "But we were just playing with Rusty."

Betsy whined, "And I love Rusty!"

Janie attempted to smooth the situation and to calm Casey and the twins. "Casey, they didn't know any better and we weren't watching them. They probably did think they were just playing with him. Look, Rusty is fine!"

Once she was sure Rusty hadn't been harmed, Casey relaxed. The twins realized they were no longer in trouble and stopped crying.

"There you go, sweetie." Casey placed Rusty back onto the floor, free of the doll clothes.

Betsy patted Rusty on the head and said, "Sorry, Rusty. I love you." Rusty licked her hand and appeared to smile at her.

Bret said, "Yeah, I'm sorry." He looked around sheepishly. "Want to play cars?"

Casey responded, "No, Bret, we have a great movie for you to watch."

"Oh, Okay!" Bret said.

They all took turns hugging. Rusty danced around the room, showing he had no hard feelings.

They moved to the living room to watch *Toy Story* and munch on popcorn. Rusty sat between Casey and Betsy. Bret positioned himself only a few feet from the television set; this was his favorite movie.

Once the movie was over, it was bedtime. Just before going to sleep, Bret excitedly shared with Janie and Casey, "I sure hope I get a Woody for my birthday!"

He seemed confused that they laughed as if he had told them something funny. Casey responded, "Bret, all the boys want a Woody!"

The girls continued to quietly giggle as they closed his door for the night. Janie said, "It's so cute when a kid says something like that so innocently."

Finally with the children in bed, exhausted Rusty and the girls tiptoed down the stairs to relax and finish the popcorn. It would've been party time, but they were too exhausted to do anything more than veg out in front of the television.

While they dialed through the list of available movies, a notice slowly scrolled across the bottom of the screen:

Body of 16-year-old Candice Bay missing teen
found at local empty house by Realtor®
Investigation suggests homicide
Details to follow on 11 o'clock news

The girls sat motionless and speechless. Casey's mind filled with dark thoughts: *No, this can't be our Tina.*

They're talking about some other teen, a stranger. Tina just ran away. Didn't she?

Janie cried, heartbroken this fate had come to her friend.

The news description of the body matched Tina's age and the location was generally close to where her family lives.

Casey's head throbbed: *Homicide? Who would kill her? Was she tortured? Did she suffer? Exactly how did she die? When?*

Both girls sat for long moments, unable to utter a word. Casey thought, *they may even know the murderer and not even realize it.* Chills ran up her spine.

Casey jumped up to re-check the locks on the doors and quickly made sure all of the windows were secure. "Janie," she said, "we're not safe."

Bret walked into the room rubbing his eyes, and Betsy came in beside him with a favorite blanket in her hand. They stood quietly, watching the girls.

Janie continued to weep; Casey began to sob.

Bret and Betsy came closer to the girls. Curious, Bret asked, "What is it?"

Casey pulled the children close to her. "We're crying for our friend, because something bad happened to her." Even though the twins didn't understand, they became sad too. Rusty tried to comfort them by jumping up and licking the children's hands.

Janie muttered, "I pray Tina didn't endure any suffering."

"Me too," Casey responded as she thought, *the innocence, the security of our beautiful community is lost!*

"Our lives will never be the same," she whispered.

Janie leaned in and they cried in each other's arms.

The twins hugged the girls, and Betsy whispered, "It'll be all right."

Soon after the news flash, Joey and his parents arrived. They had been at the local sports restaurant.

While Joey comforted the twins, his mom hugged the girls, saying, "We saw that dreadful, shocking news flash about your friend, and we got home as quickly as we could."

Joey's dad added, "Yes, we're here to support you."

Joey's mom told the girls, "I called both of your parents, and you can stay the night here, as planned, if you like. I know you're both exhausted from babysitting, it's late, and now this terrible news has surely worn you both out. We have plenty of room for you in our guest bedroom."

Janie and Casey looked at each other, then nodded agreement to stay.

"Okay now, this is the time for a group hug if ever I knew one." Joey's mom said. The group held each other tight and cried together over their loss.

Joey's dad prayed, "Lord, I don't understand how this horrible thing could happen. And I don't understand why sometimes bad things happen to good people on this earth. But I do know you are with us all right now and you will bring us through it." He continued, "We especially ask for your peace, comfort, and compassion to overflow for Tina's family and loved ones now."

"Amen," Joey and his mother said together.

After Joey's mother put the twins back to bed, the group sat quietly together for about an hour longer in the living room. Once tears had subsided, and sadness was overcome with the need for sleep, Casey and Janie thanked Joey and his parents for their support, and they all went to bed.

Chapter 9

While Casey finished her bacon and eggs, Rusty ate his serving of breakfast bacon and Casey's mom drank her coffee and read the newspaper.

Casey's mother lowered the paper. "This tragedy has no doubt devastated the entire student body at Candice Bay High School. Casey, do you know if many students will be taking advantage of the grief counseling being offered by the school administration?"

"Sure. Lots of students will go, are going. Some will pretend what happened to Tina doesn't bother them." She added, "Mom, I'm okay. If I need counseling, I'd rather talk with Pastor John or his wife."

Her mother smiled her approval. "I had no worries, Casey dear. You have plenty of options if you need to talk. I'm pleased that you'd feel comfortable turning to our pastor and our church." She paused. "Honey, I'm going to be with you at the funeral today."

Casey lowered her head. "I know. There'll be lots of people there, and many of them will be crying. I really dread it. The whole thing is so sad."

"Yes dear," her mother agreed. "It will be a terribly sad event. Her death was such a violent thing to happen, especially with her only in her teens. We'll all miss her. She grabbed Casey's hand and gently squeezed it. "Can you understand, Tina has gone to a better place, that our lives here on Earth are only temporary?"

"Yes Mom," Casey said, "I know she's gone to heaven. Did you forget? I've heard Pastor John's sermons and read the Bible for several years now."

The whole Candice Bay area turned out for Tina's funeral. Tina's parents tried to greet people as they came through the greeting line, but they were usually unable to say anything. Many of their neighbors and friends hugged them, and cried with them before moving along. Casey's family stopped to pray with the broken couple, and Joey's family joined them. Each person placed their hands on Tina's parents, and they prayed for their comfort and peace through their sadness.

Many of the students passed by Tina's parents with a hand shake, or with just a nod of their head, unsure what they were expected to do, and too emotional to talk.

Tina lay peacefully in her casket wearing a simple pale pink and cream colored gown, with a pale pink pillow under her head, and a small bouquet of matching roses lying on her chest. Anyone who had known Tina would be aware that her favorite flower was the pale pink rose.

Students came up to view her, usually in groups of two or three, or with their parents. Sometimes the weeping was hard and disturbing, so a couple of Tina's family's close neighbors stationed themselves nearby so they could quickly whisk those students away from the viewing area.

Casey and Janie went up to see Tina with their mothers. Janie cried and sobbed while Casey tried to hold most of her sorrow inside. Their mothers surrounded them with hugs and words of encouragement.

Janie blurted out to her mother, "But Mom, I wasn't a very good friend for her."

Her mother comforted her, "Janie, you're never ugly with anyone. Regardless how much you may've neglected her, caring about your own stuff like a teenager normally does, Tina always knew you as a friend of hers. That's what matters."

Casey and her mother agreed. They reminding Janie of the several times she patiently listened to Tina when she'd call late evenings while upset with her parents' fighting.

Janie smiled at them, "You know I had forgotten about that. Yeah, I was a friend to her."

Sondra and Darlene sat together, quietly whispering to each other about the décor of the funeral home and about the many flowers that were placed near Tina's casket.

"I sure hope Tina knew how much we all cared about her," Sondra said as she handed another fresh tissue to Darlene.

"Me too," Darlene choked, while she frantically

dabbed at her eyes to wipe her tears.

Joey and Mark hung back further from their families, and went up to the casket together.

Joey looked around at the flowers rather than at Tina. "Man, I hate this," he whispered.

Mark sniffed and ran his hand quickly across his cheek, mumbling, "Me too."

Jake and his parents slowly walked up to the casket and stood silently in front of it for several moments. His parents held him close while tears ran down his face. His mother passed him a tissue. He wiped his face and they proceeded to their seats, not looking at anyone in the pews.

As people were signaled to get to their seats, the pastor of the local church stood at the platform to begin his sermon. Tina's parents huddled together in their seats at the front. They collapsed in pain once the music stopped, as did their family members who sat in the two front rows. Their sobs could be heard by all. Then many of the neighbors and Tina's fellow students also began to sob.

Pastor John stretched out his arms, and began to pray. He thanked God for taking Tina up to heaven to be with Him through eternity, where she'll always be joyful and at peace. He prayed for Tina's loved ones to have comfort in knowing this.

One thing Pastor John said really affected Casey, and reminded her of her earlier conversation with her mother.

"Yes, it was a tragedy to us all, what happened to our

Tina. But I want to remind you of this: last year, in this very church, Tina accepted Christ. She was saved, dedicated her life to our Lord, and she was baptized. She is now spending eternity with God. Yes, our Tina will be greeting us at the pearly gates when we get to heaven."

Janie whispered to Casey while the sermon continued, "It would seem that we should be happy for Tina. I mean, she's now where there's no conflicts, no pain, no crying. Even though it would've been nice if she could've spent a long, full and joyful life here first."

Casey patted her friend's hand. "You're right. No reason to feel sad for her, just for ourselves. I suppose we're upset that she's left all of us. Mostly, her parents will really miss her." She paused. "I imagine they feel guilty, too, because much of their last days with her were spent bickering with each other."

"Yeah," Janie agreed. "Maybe we could go talk with her parents sometime soon. I feel a need to tell them that Tina knew they loved her no matter what may've happened before she died. And she loved them. I know this."

Casey smiled. "Of course you're right. She was sad that they couldn't seem to get along with each other. Janie, I think your message is what they need to hear."

She glanced over at Tina's pitiful parents, quietly sobbing into each other's arms. "Look how destroyed they are. You should speak with them today. They need your words of comfort."

A small group of three women from the church's choir strolled to the front to sing. They set their music on the pulpit and sang praises to God; then they sang about going home to Jesus where he has streets of gold and many mansions for each of us.

Casey whispered, "I'll go with you for support. We'll catch them alone while they're leaving the grave site."

"Thank you Casey."

For many days after the funeral, people in the close-knit community of Candice Bay remained in shock at the loss of one of their precious teenagers. Meanwhile, Casey continued to push her mother to let her resume riding her bike along the trails in the park.

"Awe, *come on* Mom," Casey said. "It's not fair that all of the teens here are kept from enjoying the things we used to do, like riding our bikes. Biking is what this place is best known for!"

Her mom responded, "It doesn't seem fair, but I'm not ready yet to let you go. Folks want to feel safe again, and we want to especially keep our teenage girls safe."

"Well, you said it," Casey added, "none of us girls are allowed out. It's like *we're* being punished."

"Just be patient, honey," her mom replied. "It'll take some time to regain a community sense of security and freedom, to recover."

"Yeah," Casey agreed. "This would all be different if we knew who killed Tina and how it happened. Mom, do you think Tina was tortured?"

"I wish I could reassure you," her mom said. "I can only hope and pray she died as peacefully as possible under the circumstances. The police are not sharing information they may have through their investigation."

"Well," Casey said, "I think we all have a right to know everything about it."

"I agree with you. We all have a stake in this." Her mom added, "But we don't want to obstruct the investigation, either, by being demanding. We'll all know the facts once the police have finished their work."

A candlelight vigil had begun after the funeral, at the empty house where Tina had been discovered. A memorial continued at that location.

One evening, like many, Janie called Casey, "Hey girl, do you want to go to the memorial tonight? Mom and Dad are going, and we have flowers to place on the porch with the flowers that others have brought."

"Yeah," Casey responded, "and I think I'll ride over with Mark and Joey. I want to ask them to keep a look-out for Tish, in case she may want to make good on her threat at the P.E. fight."

"Oh, you're right! They promised to be your body guards when we told them about her threat," Janie recalled.

"They'll be watching out for Butch, too, you know." Casey paused. "I have a few candles for us to light. Meet you at 7 o'clock?"

"Okay, I'll see you there."

Janie and Casey quickly found each other once they had arrived at Tina's memorial site. They stood and looked around at the crowd with the many flowers that were neatly in place on the porch.

"Oh my, look at how many sad teenagers are here in honor of Tina," Casey commented.

"Yeah," Janie responded, "and I bet Tina had no idea how many of us care about her." She paused, "I mean, *cared* about her."

Both girls began to cry. Janie's parents walked over and hugged them.

While Janie's mother held her hand on the shoulder of each of the girls, she whispered, "I know this is terribly hard for you." She paused a second to ensure that her voice didn't reveal her own sad emotions. "Please know that Tina is in a wonderful place now, and she has no fear, suffering, or pain."

"I know, Momma," Janie said tearfully.

Janie's dad whispered a short prayer while the four of them stood together.

Mr. Curtis was at the memorial site for a short time and briefly hugged Janie. Meanwhile, Mark and Joey quietly walked around the area.

Joey noticed Tish looking at Casey from several yards away, so he moved closer to Casey while he signaled Mark to do the same. Janie also noticed Tish looking at Casey and immediately froze.

"Casey," Janie whispered as she grabbed Casey's arm and pointed in Tish's direction.

"Oh Janie, I saw her when we first got here," Casey said. "We've been taking turns eyeing each other."

Tish and Casey caught each other's attention. At first they glared at each other. Tish made a slight nod and turned away, not looking in Casey's direction again.

"Well," Casey said, "I assume this is Tish's way of trying to get past the fight."

"I hope you're right," Janie said. "But there were no apologies."

Mark and Joey had the same assumption when they saw Tish nod and leave, and they moved on to talk with some of their friends. The girls watched them go.

"That's fine with me," Casey responded. "At least I don't have to worry about being broken in half!" They both laughed; relieved they no longer had to be concerned about Tish's threat.

Soon after, Casey noticed Butch but pretended not to see him; Janie didn't seem to be aware he was nearby. *Geez,* Casey thought, *isn't it enough just to be here, without having to face all the other issues, too?*

Butch had his eyes on Casey. He slowly maneuvered through the crowd and stood quietly beside her, waiting for her to acknowledge his presence.

"Butch, what are you doing here? We don't want to talk to you!"

Butch responded in such a polite tone and manner that it surprised her. He directed his response to the both of them, and Janie turned to face him.

"I want to apologize to you both for constantly being such a douchebag and especially to you, Janie, for attacking you like I did. I don't know why I did that, but it won't ever happen again."

The girls looked at each other and back to him, as he continued with his explanation. Casey considered, *really? I've never heard him speak in such a calm and intelligent tone before. Maybe he rehearsed this?*

Butch continued, "I guess I liked to show off to the others, and it got out of hand.

Anyway, my dad and I had a very long and serious talk about all of this, and I have to agree with him. This bully attitude doesn't jibe with my college plans at all. I really do want to succeed in college somewhere, and later on become successful in business management like my dad." He waited for a reaction, but the girls had nothing to say.

Casey took mental note; *this sounds more like a speech his dad would make than something Butch would say. Like, when did he ever mention college plans?*

Butch cleared his throat. "I still have time to change my ways, change my attitude," he grimaced, "and friends, so I can do what I want with my future. So my family has decided, and I agree, it's time for us to be moving on. In a new environment, I can have a fresh start and this time to get it right."

Casey was so relieved to hear that he planned to move away. *Surely Janie's as happy as I am. We're just not being obvious.* Casey said, "Well, Butch, if you mean all of this, then I accept your apology and I hope your new start will work out for you."

Janie added timidly, "I hope so too, Butch. I wish you well."

"Well then, see ya." Butch tilted his head in farewell, and walked away.

"Well," Casey said, "that was different. I didn't know he had it in him."

Janie confided to Casey that she has been afraid of Butch after the locker incident.

Casey hesitated and spoke quietly after looking around to make sure nobody was within earshot. "Do you think he could've had anything to do with Tina's death?"

Janie responded, "I don't know."

"Yeah." Casey said. "Even if he didn't–and I hope he didn't have anything to do with it—I'm so glad he's moving away!"

"Casey, when he had me pinned, he had such a scary look on his face, like he was crazy!"

Casey nodded agreement, "Yeah, I thought so too."

They said together, "Good riddance!"

Casey sat down at the dinner table next to her brother at Joey's house. Her family had come over for the evening after church service.

Joey's dad opened the local newspaper and after he turned the page, he announced, "Hey everybody." Once he had the group's attention, he continued, "The police department is finally sharing some information about Tina."

Joey's dad skimmed the article, "Investigators say the autopsy findings revealed Tina had been killed through blunt-force trauma to the head, dying instantly. They believed this happened the same night she disappeared. They could not determine exactly when the body was moved to the empty house, only that it was moved there within five days of its discovery. Before then, the local Realtor had taken folks through the house for shows. Police found no signs of forced entry."

Casey began to cry, and her mom stood up from the

table and walked over to Casey. She leaned over from behind and gave her a hug.

Joey's mom whispered, "Lord, help us all!"

"Oh my," Casey's dad said, "at least this news doesn't sound like she had physical suffering before she died. Does it say anything about Butch or Jake being persons of interest?"

"No," responded Joey's dad, "but that's what I understand from the rumors going around."

Casey's mom added, "Tina's parents were also interviewed several times. Maybe they were potential suspects, but that doesn't seem to make any sense."

"Oh, I think that's just routine," said Casey's dad.

Joey's mom spoke up, "You know, I just want all of this to be behind us, so our teens can get over what happened. As it is, they seem to feel guilty whenever they do let go and are carefree and happy."

Joey snapped, "Well geez, Mom. How can we move on at this point, knowing one of our own was killed and the murderer is still out there! Maybe he's even living in our area!"

Mark pat his cousin on the shoulder. "Yeah, we all feel frustration, but we have no reason to get angry. Police are working hard on this, and they won't stop until the culprit is found and punished."

Except for the twins happily playing at the swing set, everyone sat in silence as they meditated on this new information about Tina. Each knew the truth of it: this could've happened to any of them and they may never know who did it.

Meanwhile, Janie was helping her mother serve

dinner for her father and their guest, Mr. Curtis. It was a southern meal, with pinto beans, fried potatoes, sausage with onions, applesauce and homemade cornbread. Mr. Curtis had mentioned one day that he'd never had a southern-cooked meal. They all held hands while Janie's father said the blessing.

"So how do you like it?" Janie's mother asked, after watching Mr. Curtis take several bites.

"Well now, this is delicious," announced Mr. Curtis while he positioned another spoonful of beans close to his mouth. "It's absolutely delicious!"

Mr. Curtis and Janie's father discussed politics while Janie and her mother silently ate their food.

Janie wasn't paying attention to what the men were saying. She was daydreaming about Jake, how nice it would've been if only nothing had happened to Tina. Suddenly, Janie caught the end of a statement her father had made, something about Jake. She listened while her father and Mr. Curtis talked.

"Yes, I did see Jake and Tina arguing that night, and I believe she was crying. I had to tell the police about what I saw and heard, once they had stopped by to ask me if I knew anything about her where-abouts that night." He paused and loaded his plate with another serving of fried potatoes. He smiled at Janie's mother, "This is certainly the best meal I've had in a long time."

Janie's dad wrinkled his forehead, "I just can't picture Jake involved in anything to do with Tina's demise." He looked toward his wife to see if she agreed.

"I don't believe he had anything to do with it, either. He seems like such a fine young man," Janie's mother agreed, nodding her head at her husband.

"Well, whatever happened, the police with find it all out eventually," Janie's dad said, abruptly dismissing the topic.

"Honey, will you pass me the cornbread? It's exceptionally good this time. Did you do something different?"

Janie's mother smiled at her husband, "I just added another egg, to make it more cake-like. I'll fix it like that more often, now that I know you like it that way."

"Yes, please do. Thank you."

Once it appeared that the others had finished eating, Janie volunteered to clear the table while her mother made dessert offerings.

Mr. Curtis and Janie's dad each wanted a small serving of vanilla ice cream.

Janie looked pleadingly at her mother, "Mom, can I be excused? I don't really want a dessert tonight."

"Yes dear, go ahead and get yourself set up for school tomorrow."

Janie kissed her mother and walked around the table and hugged her dad. She looked over at Mr. Curtis, and grinned, "Good night Mr. Curtis."

Mr. Curtis tipped his head and responded, "Good night Janie-dear."

As soon as Janie got to her room, she shut the door and grabbed her cell.

"Jake? I'm sorry I couldn't call until now. We had Mr. Curtis over for dinner, and I couldn't get away."

"Not a problem! I was helping Mom clean up the

pantry anyway."

Jake paused. "While we were cleaning, Mom told me that there was a lot of talk at the school's board meeting about grief counselling."

"What about it?"

"Apparently some of the parents are not satisfied that the school is doing all that they should be doing for grieving students."

"Well you know Jake, it's just going to take some time for us all to get over the shock of what's happened to Tina."

Jake signed, "That's what they know. But to appease the complaining parents, the principal's going to hold an assembly meeting tomorrow for the entire student body. He will emphasize, again, the importance of grief counselling and that the school is offering it to students."

Janie looked down, "Maybe that's a good idea. I think if I go to counseling, it might help me deal with Tina's death better."

Jake shrugged, "Yeah. It seems like everyone's bummed out about it. Like everyone seems sad. You know?"

The couple didn't speak for a few minutes. Janie considered telling him what Mr. Curtis and her parents had said at the dinner table about Jake, but she decided not to bring that subject up.

Then Jake spoke, "Oh yeah, I almost forgot. I think the school board also made a decision about the class graduation. It's gonna be small, and in July sometime."

"That sounds right, doesn't it? I mean, under the

circumstances," Janie said.

"Yeah. I'm just glad it isn't our graduating class this year."

Janie lay down on her bed while Jake yawned from his bedroom. Then he cleared his throat, "I already told you that I can't sneak out to see you tonight. But I sure wish that I could. I'd love to hold you."

Janie giggled, "We'll just have to make sure that happens very soon, now won't we?" She smiled and hugged herself at the thought of him holding her.

"Well. Good night my sweetheart. Love you."

"I love you too, Jake." Then they both made kissing sounds on the cell, a habit they had formed some time ago.

Chapter 10

The School Board decided the Candice Bay High School's 125 graduates would have a small ceremony on the second Saturday in July in their fairly new auditorium. It was believed that attendance would be low because graduates could opt out of attending and still get their diploma.

Mark attended the ceremony, as did his family and Joey's family, his Aunt Grace and Granny who all lived in the Richmond area, and his grandparents on his dad's side.

When Casey sat in the audience beside Bret, he excitedly whispered to her, "Mark is wearing a dress!" he began laughing.

"Bret, that's his graduation gown. Every graduate is wearing one."

She smiled during the ceremony, thinking about the dresses everyone on stage was wearing. *He's such a cutie-pie. These kids are not monster twins after all.* Casey realized she just had to get used to children.

At the same moment, she looked over at Betsy, sitting straight up like a little angel, with her pretty floral dress smoothed out, holding her shiny white purse in her lap. Casey thought, *she's a cutie-pie too, but these twins sure aren't much alike.*

As promised, the speeches were short and filled with promises for the graduates' future. The principal spoke a few moments in honor of Tina, and quickly finished about hope and faith as a positive beginning for the graduates. Awards were given for various scholastic accomplishments. Finally, the graduates were called by name to receive their diploma and shake hands with the principal.

Mark's family was filled with pride as they watched Mark walk across the stage. The family and Mark's friends yelled, "YEAH Mark! We love you!"

Belinda announced to her family seated in her row, "Excuse me folks, I need to get in the aisle so I can snap some good shots of my son," and she carefully scooted along to the isle.

"Oh, I'm right with you," replied Joey's mother with her camera in hand, and she scooted along the row as well.

Once in the aisle, the two women hugged. Belinda said, "I'm so proud of him!" They were both emotional and teary-eyed, causing some of the others to get emotional, too.

"Here Belinda." Joey's mother handed her a tissue. Belinda dabbed her eyes.

After the ceremony had finished and family and friends congratulated Mark, his dad asked, "Hey, who wants to go with us for a nice steak dinner?"

Before the group began to eat, Mark and Casey's dad

proposed a toast. "This is to my son, a fine young man, whom I'm very proud of. May God bless and protect him in all that he does in his future." He paused and looked at his son with adoration. "I love you son."

During the meal, Casey saw Steve. He was also with a large group.

Oh my God! she thought, *he's looking at me!*

Steve casually walked to her table. "Hi Casey," he said, smiling and looking her over. "I guess your family's celebrating a graduate, too."

"Yeah," Casey nervously adjusted her hair and smiled. "My brother," pointing at Mark.

Steve leaned in and placed his hand on Casey's shoulder. "My cousin," pointing at a pretty girl with his family group.

As he pointed they noticed the waiter was serving the food to Steve's family. Steve gently squeezed her shoulder. "See ya soon," and he rejoined his group.

Casey mumbled, "Yeah, sure," while thinking, *he spoke to me, he knows my name AND he said he'll see me soon! I'm in heaven!* Casey resumed eating calmly but her mind was racing.

Steve walked over to Casey and her family's table, and shyly tapped her on the shoulder. She turned to see him grinning at her. Elated, yet embarrassed (because he did this in front of her family), she smiled up at him.

He whispered, "Casey, I've had a crush on you for months. Will you please go out to dinner and a movie with me? Sometime soon?"

Breathless, she tried to answer, but her mouth was too dry to speak. She quickly gulped half of her glass of water. "Oh yes, Steve. Yes!" as she placed her glass onto her silverware and water spilled into her plate of food. Unaware of this accident, he smiled at her adoringly, and gently rested his hand on her cheek. He leaned down as if he planned to kiss her face. Panicked, she said, "No, no! not in front of my dad!"

"Casey? Hello?" Joey said.

Casey quickly pulled out of her daydream. "Um. Yeah?"

Her mother said, "I've asked you twice to pass me the napkins."

"Sorry." Casey mumbled, passing the napkins to her mother.

Joey gave her a gentle punch with his elbow. "Wonder where *you* were," he laughed, glancing over at Steve's table.

Casey mentally noted, *and poof! There goes my Steve again.*

The next morning, Mark caught Casey in the kitchen. "Hey sis, I want to ask you about something."

"Yeah?" Casey continued pouring herself a glass of orange juice. "What?"

"I have a friend, a senior now, who needs help with science. He's afraid he won't pass. I thought of you, since you're good in that. He'd pay something if you would tutor him some this summer. What do you think?"

Casey thought about the extra money. "Well, yeah, I'd consider tutoring. Who is it?"

Mark explained, "Its Adam. He's been here before, working on my car with me."

"Oh. I remember him." Casey also recalled Adam as really nice looking. She had hoped to meet him. She smiled. "Sure, bring him over and introduce us."

"I will," Mark said, "real soon."

Casey and Rusty lay in her bed one morning while Casey pondered all that had happened before the school year ended, and during the summer so far.

I wonder about Janie. For a while, she was always here evenings, watching movies and eating dinner. She was like a part of our family. Now what?

What's different? I guess we need to have a serious girl talk. I want us to continue as best friends. No changes! If our parents weren't so worried about a killer out there, we could enjoy the summer like we used to: swimming, soccer, and bike riding.

Casey picked up her phone and called Janie. "Hey girl, what've you been up to?"

"Hi Casey," Janie cheerfully responded, "oh, nothing much."

"Well I was thinking," Casey said, "how about we go to the library and sign up for the summer book club? It's not too late, you know, and we always enjoy it."

"Hey, Casey, that's a very good idea!" Janie said.

So Casey rode her bike over to Janie's house.

They laughed together while riding to the library, glad to be able to get back to something that they had enjoyed doing.

"You know Casey, I didn't realize I missed riding my

bike so much!"

"Yeah," Casey responded, "actually, it was my mom's idea. She said we'd gone long enough without having fun riding our bikes. But she did emphasize we be very careful."

"Well, this is just the beginning, girlfriend!"

"You're so right!" Casey said, and she sped up ahead of Janie by a few yards. Then she waited for Janie to catch up. "It looks like we might've gotten out of shape some, too." They both laughed.

Once they reached the library, they parked the bikes in their usual spot and entered the building.

When they were younger, they both loved adventure stories, but during the past year, Janie's tastes had been leaning toward romance novels, while Casey preferred the mysteries.

"So Janie, what've you been up to lately? You haven't been coming to my house for a while now." Janie quickly looked at the pile of books in her hands, mostly romance novels, as if studying something on the front covers.

"Janie?" Casey pondered over her friend's silence. "Hey, you can say anything to me. What is it?" Janie seemed embarrassed.

"Well, Tina's death hurt us all, but especially, it was very heart-breaking for Jake. He really loved her, and he's been seriously depressed over all this, and now with the investigation going on and not producing anything..."

"I didn't realize you've been talking with Jake at all. At least, not since you spoke with him when Tina had disappeared. How long has this been goin' on?"

Janie's face flushed. "Well, you know I called him the night she disappeared. I guess we chatted every now and again after that. When she was found dead, we began talking more, since both of us, well, we were hurting."

"Why didn't you tell me, Janie?"

"Because the police keep questioning him. I guess he's still a person of interest, and maybe he will stay that way for a long time since they have nothing much else to go on."

She paused and grabbed Casey's hand, confronting her face to face, "I know he had nothing to do with Tina's disappearance. He is innocent. He has been heartbroken and depressed since the day she disappeared."

"We don't *know* that he's innocent, Janie, but I don't think he's a cold-blooded killer, either."

Casey looked at Janie's expression with knowing eyes. "Oh my goodness. I think you're in love with him." She sat quietly for a few moments. "Are you?"

Janie's eyes welled up. She nodded.

"But what does he think of you? Are you just his friend that he can talk about Tina to?"

Janie wrung her hands. "No. It started that way, but now I think he cares about me, too."

Casey looked again at her friend with compassion. *Surely Janie knows that hooking up with Jake right now could be a dumb move. Jake, Butch, and maybe even Tina's parents are their only suspects. Jake could be the one!* Casey could almost imagine Jake accidently hurting her, and then she unexpectedly died. He would try to hide the body, and when that didn't work, he might make it look like a mad man had done it by dumping her body into that empty house for discovery.

Because Casey valued their friendship, she felt the need to caution Janie about the remote possibility that Jake may hurt her. Casey approached her friend seriously. "Janie, I want you to promise me something, okay?"

"Yeah, what is it?" Janie asked.

"I want you to promise to be alert at all times to what Jake is saying, doing, and to any changes in his emotions while you're talking to him on the phone and especially when you're with him. Can you?"

"Geez, Casey, it sounds like you want me to spy on him." Janie was not happy with this request, but she was willing to listen, knowing Casey had her best interests at heart.

"No, it's not spying on him," Casey explained. "You're simply being aware of what's going on around you, paying attention to what's happening with someone you're with. Do you understand?"

Janie sighed. "Yes, I understand. Is that all?"

"No," Casey said. "I also want you to have a plan in mind whenever you're with him. What can you do, and where can you go if he should suddenly start acting strange."

Janie frowned, but Casey kept on pushing her point. Casey told herself, *Mom would be proud of me for this!*

"Janie, this is how it has to be for girls anyway. When we're older, out on our own and dating, we're going to still have to be careful—just like that."

"Oh yeah, I know where some of this is coming from. You're remembering that movie we watched. What was the title?" Janie continued, "Mmm, I can't remember. But anyway, the women had a dating system. They would call each other and leave messages as to where they were going and with whom."

Casey thought about it. "Maybe good advice? When we're older, maybe that's something we can think about doing."

Janie gave Casey a hug. "I understand what you're sayin' and I appreciate your concern. I do promise I will be watchful and careful when I'm with him, even though I believe Jake is trustworthy."

"Okay, great," Casey said, relieved that she was able to get through to her friend without getting her mad about it.

Janie was also relieved, and she thanked Casey for her concern about her welfare.

"Janie, I guess I can understand your need to keep your relationship a secret right now," she said. "Under the circumstances, that seems to be a smart way to be."

Janie responded, "It's hard. Even though I'm sure he had nothing at all to do with the murder, I still feel kind of guilty."

"Guilty?" Casey studied this. "Oh, you mean for taking Tina's boyfriend?"

"Well yeah, that, but also because I always felt he was too good for her. I guess I always had a sort of crush on him."

"Oh." Casey mulled this over. *Well, I thought she had*

a crush on him. I got a big hint when she spoke about Jake that day we heard of Tina's disappearance. It's so unusual for Janie to say bad stuff about someone.

"But you're only human with how you felt. It isn't like you ever did anything to sabotage their relationship, and you didn't go around talking bad about her, either."

Janie reflected on her past behavior. "You're right. There was more I could've done for her, but I believe I was a good friend to Tina."

"Janie, you were a good friend of hers, despite your personal feelings about Jake. I don't see any reason for you to feel guilty because he's now interested in you."

"Maybe it's because I feel so bad about what happened to her, but sometimes it feels wrong that I can now be happy with him."

"But don't you remember? Janie, you told me that she started smokin' weed and they fought often because he didn't want to do it. Actually, I don't think he liked to drink, either."

Janie appeared confused, apparently wondering where she was going with this.

"Don't you see? They weren't a match anymore. It was only a matter of time before she dumped him. She was looking for something to make her feel better, and he wasn't enough."

Janie's face brightened. "You're so right! They were bound to quit anyway. Yeah!"

Casey continued, "And you know what Janie? I think Tina would want us all to move on with our lives."

"Yes!" Janie agreed. "Remember her, but still be happy with our own lives. Move on!"

"But you still might be right to hide it that you're hanging out with him, for a while anyway. Even though you don't believe Jake had anything to do with Tina's death, he's a suspect."

"Oh yeah, I know. You don't need to remind me. But it feels so much better without having the guilt. You know?"

They hugged briefly.

"Okay, girlfriend," Casey said. "Let's get serious about these books! We're gonna be book club winners again this year!"

Janie laughed in agreement.

That evening Mark introduced Adam to Casey. Mark walked into the living room with Adam, and Casey looked up from the television show she'd been watching and walked over to greet them.

"So Casey, this is Adam. Adam, Casey," Mark said.

The moment Adam and Casey looked into each other's eyes, they were awestruck.

Adam stammered, "Hi Casey," putting his hand out.

"Hi Adam," Casey said. *Oh Geez, you're so hot!*

Mark looked at the couple, still holding hands, and he smiled. "Well, I'll leave you two alone." And he walked out of the room unnoticed.

Casey turned the television off. She and Adam sat together on the couch. They discussed their tutoring arrangements. Before he left, they hugged, and then they giggled.

Casey marveled, *this was our first meeting and we're already hugging!*

That night Casey had a wonderful dream about her and Adam double dating with Janie and Jake. They rode in Adam's metallic blue Convertible on a bright summer day to the beach. She could see them laughing and singing as the wind blew through their hair. The radio was turned on full blast, playing the latest tunes.

Janie hugged Jake, "I'm so happy the police found out that Tina wasn't killed after all. She died of natural causes."

"Yes," Casey said, "And she didn't suffer at all."

Adam smiled at Casey, "and I'm so thankful that Mark introduced me to my beautiful girlfriend." Casey giggled.

They continued singing while they rode down the highway for a while. The weather was perfect and the sky was clear and sunny. They pulled over at a nice rest stop for a picnic lunch. Casey's mother had packed drinks, sandwiches, chips and brownies. Once the meal had been laid out on their picnic table, the group gathered around to start eating. But Adam leaned over and began nibbling on Casey's ear.

Casey giggled, "Oh stop that, Adam!" but he kept nibbling. She giggled loudly, "Oh, that tickles!"

Casey woke up to see Rusty licking her ear. "Oh shoot, Rusty. You sure ruined a good dream." He whimpered and gently pushed his nose into her shoulder. He waited a few moments, then did it again.

"Okay! I get it!" Casey got up and Rusty jumped off the bed. She headed down the stairs, with Rusty scampering ahead of her. "Good thing you don't need to go potty every night, my little friend."

Chapter 11

That night after dark, Janie slipped out of her house to meet Jake again. They quietly walked hand in hand to the nearby cul-de-sac common grounds, an area filled with trees. This was a tiny step forward in their relationship.

"Jake, I believe it was inevitable that Tina and you would break up."

"Yes, I guess so." Jake paused, "She was unhappy about her parents, and I couldn't seem to get her to think about us, our relationship. All she wanted to do is brood, drink, and experiment with drugs. I had started to dread talking with her. I felt trapped, because I didn't want to drop her while she was so unhappy."

"I'm so sorry," Janie responded. She admired Jake for being willing to go through some rough spots with Tina, while he tried to be a nice, supportive friend to her.

"But Jake, I believe Tina would've wanted us to go on with our lives. What do you think?"

Jake nodded in agreement, "Yes, that's true. She was a nice girl, not selfish. If we'd had time to break up before she disappeared, she wouldn't have been ugly about it. Not with me, and not with you." He smiled at Janie, and squeezed her hand.

With these ideas out in the open, the couple finally felt freed from guilt over their own relationship, and that seemed to give them some peace and comfort.

"Ah, my Janie," he said, "you are my heart, my love. I'm yours."

Janie smiled with adoration, her heart beating loudly in her chest, "I love you. I'm devoted to you, only you." They hugged each other, and she looked up into his eyes.

"Someday, not now with this case going on and I'm not yet cleared, but once it's done, I want us to be together for everyone to see." He continued, "Finally, since this whole mess started with Tina's disappearance, I feel happy and free." He smiled at Janie, and rested his hand on her face.

"So do I, Jake," Janie responded. "All my sadness and pain seems to be lifting, being replaced with my love for you."

Jake hugged Janie close. "Can you imagine us going to college together?"

Janie kissed Jake lightly on the lips and whispered, "Oh yes, Jake, that's what I want, too."

Then she tilted her head, "You know, Casey and I talk about college often. Do you know yet what you'd like to get into?"

"Oh I don't know. I think I'd like to get business administration under my belt, but I'm actually interested in maybe becoming a veterinarian."

"Well," Janie said thoughtfully, "If you had your own business as a veterinarian, it would be useful to have a business background."

Jake smiled, I hadn't looked at it that way. So there's not really such a conflict."

He ran his fingers through her hair, "Janie, you're a smart cookie. Good looks *and* brains. I'm a lucky guy."

Janie giggled with happiness, but she was too embarrassed to respond. Instead, she smiled and patted his shoulder.

"And Jake, to be a veterinarian, you'll need a background in the medical field, like I will be doing. We could be taking some of the same first-year medical courses together."

"That would be great! We'll have to plan on it."

He walked Janie back to her porch, where the moonlight fell onto their silhouettes as he held her tenderly, and they kissed. Their kissing was soft and warm, even passionate.

Suddenly, they were interrupted by a cat's screech and what sounded like the banging from a trash can or it's lid. Jake kissed Janie one more time, most tenderly and with promise.

"I love you, my little angel." Jake said.

Janie looked into his eyes. "I love you, too," she said, and gave him one more kiss.

Then he left while she watched him from her porch.

Jake meandered on his way home savoring the memory of their kisses. For the first time in a very long time, he was happy, and hopeful for a future with his Janie.

He was free to love her, for the rest of their lives if they wanted to. He softly whistled a little tune, filled with hopes and dreams.

About an hour after Jake had left Janie's house, someone quietly walked down the sidewalk toward her house, which was now quiet with no lights on.

This person was dressed completely in black. He very carefully, quietly, and slowly padded his way up the front steps and onto the porch. Slowly and deliberately, he pulled a tool out of his pocket, and then, very swiftly, he cut the chain to Janie's bike. He placed the chain and the tool back into his pocket. Without a sound, he grabbed the bike and lifted it. Then he carried the bike with him back into the night.

Early the next morning Janie's dad put on his work attire and grabbed his briefcase. Before he could get to the front door, his wife came out from the kitchen.

He said to Janie's mother, "Honey, you didn't need to get up with me."

His wife smiled lovingly while she handed him a thermos of coffee. "I wanted to send you off. I know you appreciate my efforts."

"I'll only be at the office for a few hours," her husband responded. They kissed and hugged.

As Janie's dad opened the door, he immediately noticed the bike was missing. "What the hell!" He paused. Then he yelled into the house, "Well, now, he's finally done it! We're calling the police! I can't take this shit anymore!"

His wife came running. "What is it dear?"

Her husband responded sarcastically, "Do you see anything missing?"

Janie pulled the door further open to see what the fuss was about. "Oh NO!" She angrily looked at her father, "Really, Dad! Right off the porch?"

Her mother sighed. "This is frightening, that someone would be so bold as to take something, our child's bike, from our porch at night."

"I'm not a child!" Janie retorted.

"Maybe we wasted our time and money moving from New York," said her dad.

"Oh, don't ever say that, dear. Candice Bay is much better than the neighborhood we lived in," she said, in her effort to lessen the blow of this personal theft, "We'll get through this, and at least nobody tried to physically harm us."

Janie mumbled, "Oh, now I get it." She paused. "No wonder I was amazed to hear his apology. It was all lies just to keep me off-balance. He just wanted to prevent me from pressing charges."

"What are you talking about, sweetheart?" her dad asked, more concerned than angry.

Janie explained, "One time early this summer, while we were at Tina's memorial, Butch came up to Casey and me."

"Butch? What'd HE want?" her dad asked. "I knew we should've gotten a peace-bond on that boy!"

"Well, he actually apologized to us, especially to me." Janie paused.

Her mom tried to calm her husband, and grasped

his arm. "Now sweetheart, please listen to her for a minute."

Janie continued, "Dad, it wasn't to be ugly, Butch had said he was sorry and that it'd never happen again. In fact, they're moving out of town."

She looked at the blank space on the porch. "I was all ready to give him the benefit of the doubt and wipe the slate clean, but now I think it was all a lot of crap."

Janie looked at her parents, sorry they've had to go through so much sadness because of her. Now her bike had been stolen.

Still agitated, her dad agreed. "I'm with you. He had his retaliation planned out when he spoke with you. Well, I'm not allowing any more of this. I'm reporting his ass to the police right now."

With deliberate gestures, he slammed his briefcase down and dialed the cell phone.

Chapter 12

Janie was distraught that someone would steal her bike, especially because of the timing of it. For one thing, she wondered if God was punishing her for taking Tina's boyfriend. She quickly dismissed that idea. Also, here it was only days after she and Casey had again started riding. With no bike during the summer, she potentially would be left out of many fun riding adventures with her friend.

While the police office took down information from Janie's parents, she called Casey.

"What? Are you kidding me?" Casey shouted when Janie had told her about the theft. *I thought things would finally calm down by now, but then this!*

Mark overheard Casey shouting. "What's going on, Casey?"

Casey quickly held her hand over the cell while she told Mark what she'd been told. "That's all I know," she concluded.

While Mark stood by listening, Casey said to Janie, "Hey, Mark and I will be right over."

"Thanks," Janie said, "see you soon."

Casey's mom walked into the room. "What's going on? What were you yelling about? Where are you two going?"

"Mom," Mark explained, "Janie's bike was stolen last night, right off their front porch."

"Yeah," Casey said. "We want to be supportive for Janie."

"Oh my goodness!" their mother exclaimed. "Sure, sure. Go comfort your friend. We'll talk more about this later."

Mark parked his Mustang at the curb in front of Janie's house, and they walked over to where Janie stood in the yard.

Janie smiled at her friends. "Thank you for coming," she whispered. "The police officer is writing a report." She pointed at the officer talking with her parents.

Casey patted Janie's hand, and Mark slung his arm over Janie's shoulder. "It'll all work out, Janie. You'll see," Mark said.

They listened to the police officer for a while and watched him shake each of Janie's parent's hands.

"Thank you, Mr. and Mrs. Smith, you've been most helpful," the officer said. "Someone from our office will get back with you when we have anything to tell you."

"Great, officer, and thank you for your time," said Janie's dad.

Once the police officer left, Janie's dad and mom shared that the police would check around, but they didn't have much to go on unless a neighbor had witnessed the theft or anyone hanging around their house last night.

Janie immediately looked down, biting her lip with worry.

Both of Janie's parents rushed to her side, hugging her and assuring that it would be all right.

Mark and Casey looked on. Then Mark suggested, "Hey, Mr. Smith, we haven't had breakfast yet and if it's okay with you, I'd like to take Janie and sis out to eat. How does that sound?"

Janie smiled while her mother said, "Oh, Mark. What a fine young man you are."

Janie's dad glanced at Janie and her mother and they nodded. "Sure Mark. Thank you. You're a nice fella."

Mark and the girls quickly walked to his Mustang, and he drove them off.

Janie's dad turned to his wife, "I've already called the office and there's no point in my going in for only a few hours. I can work from home." He sighed. "What are we going to do about Janie's bike? We can't afford to replace it right now. Can we?"

Janie's mother wrung her hands, "Regardless, honey, I think we should try. You see how much she's been through, and this loss really hurts."

"Well," her husband replied, "go ahead and research websites for a good deal. If we're to do this, I want her to have a nice replacement since she spends so much of her time riding a bike."

"I agree," his wife happily responded, and she began her research.

She quickly found a good deal. Janie's mother rushed to her husband's side in his office. "Honey,

I found something that might work for us. A white, lightweight GT Road Bike, valued at $1,000."

"What?" Her husband looked up from his work. "That's rather high, isn't it?"

"No dear, it's on sale through this weekend for $700," she proudly announced.

"Well. In that case, make the deal and arrange for me to pick it up Monday morning, on the way to work." He paused. "Thank you, dear."

During the afternoon, the police officer called Janie's parents. They set it up as a conference call. The officer explained, "Mr. and Mrs. Smith, I want to assure you that we take this theft seriously. We checked out your alleged thief and he has a solid alibi. Butch was spending the evening yesterday with his parents at a family rehearsal dinner. The restaurant confirmed."

Janie's dad responded, "Thank you, officer, for getting back with us so quickly. I had thought Butch was good for it."

His wife said, "Yes, thank you. I guess I'm glad it wasn't Butch. But I don't have any idea who else it could've been."

"Me either," her husband added.

The officer said, "We have no other leads or information regarding this theft. At this point, our investigation will remain inactive unless we receive further information we can investigate. If not, our case will eventually be closed regarding this matter."

Janie's parents accepted the officer's statement, believing they had received fair treatment.

Later in the afternoon Casey and Adam seriously studied two chapters in his science book for a solid hour at the library, but once it started getting close to dinner time, he offered to walk her home.

Adam didn't attempt to hold her hand because he wasn't sure she'd like that, although he knew she liked him. Instead, he frequently placed his hand on her shoulder as they walked. She seemed to enjoy him doing it.

Adam glanced at Casey, "So how do you think I'm doing? I mean, do you think we'll be able to cover everything before school starts?"

"Oh yeah, no problem Adam. You're not having nearly the trouble with the subject matter as you may think."

"Really?" Adam smiled.

She smiled up at him, "Really."

"Well, in that case, maybe we could hang out together. You know, go to a movie, or something else that's fun once in a while?"

Casey told herself, *Yes, yes, YES! But play it cool. Don't let him know how excited you are.*

"Humm. Maybe we should first make sure we're getting the work done as we've scheduled."

Adam touched her hair, "Well now, that sounds like incentive. Sorta." They both laughed.

They carefully walked around a bike that was parked on the sidewalk, that was only a few yards from her home.

"Since you'll already be at my house, how about having dinner with us? That is, if you don't have other plans. My folks would be glad to have you."

Adam gave Casey's arm a gentle squeeze, "Yes, that would be great. I just need to call my mom to let her know."

"Maybe we could watch something on T.V. too?"

"I'd love to! Would this be kinda like our first date?"

The couple smiled at each other. *He's so easy to have fun with!* Casey noted to herself. *I think he and I are really compatible.*

"Umm. I think we should count it as our first date sometime when we go out by ourselves," She paused to touch his shoulder and look into his eyes, smiling, "and you put more effort into it."

"Oh, of course," Adam laughed, "and Casey, that means you've already said yes! Ha ha! Do you like that idea of going to the movie theater?"

"Sure."

Adam wrinkled his brow, "Do you like to go swimming?"

"Are you kidding? I practically have gills!"

"Well then," Adam said, "Maybe we could get a few others to go swimming with us. We have plenty of fantastic summer weather left."

"Yes. I really like that idea."

She opened the front door and they walked into the living room. Rusty ran in from the kitchen to greet them.

Adam reached his hand down to pet Rusty while Casey went into the kitchen to tell her mother that she wanted Adam to have dinner with them.

"Oh Casey, I'm so sorry, but your father and I already

made plans for us tonight." She paused, noting Casey's disappointment. She hugged her daughter. "Please tell Adam that we have family plans tonight, but we certainly welcome him to have dinner with us another time."

Casey shared the news with Adam, "I'm sorry. I should've checked before suggesting it."

He took it cheerily, "Not a problem. I'll take your mom up on that future invite."

Casey walked Adam to the front door, and slipped out onto the porch with him. She quietly shut the door behind her. He went down one step, and turned to face her. Quickly, he kissed her on the cheek. They locked hands and he kissed her in the mouth.

They both giggled. "See ya soon, "he said, and they hugged.

"Yes, soon, " Casey said, smiling from ear to ear. After he had walked to the sidewalk, he turned and they waved good-bye to each other.

Casey watched Adam until he'd walked out of sight. Then she went into the house. *I think I have a boyfriend. Yep. I think he's my boyfriend.*

On Monday evening, Janie was surprised to find a new bike sitting on the front porch for her, with a big red bow attached to it.

"Oh Mom, Dad!" she squealed. "This is the best bike in all of Candice Bay!" Janie hugged and kissed her parents.

It took a few minutes for Janie's parents to show her all of the details and features to her new bike. She eagerly listened.

Janie grasped the handlebars, saying, "Um. Mom, Dad. Could I..."

Before she could complete her sentence, her parents both nodded. "Yes dear," Janie's mother said. "You can ride it over to Casey's. After all, I'm sure she's endured much of your whining over the lost bike. She should be a part of your happiness, too."

Quickly, Janie rode off toward her friend's house.

"Hey, look what I've got! What do you think of it?" she beamed proudly after she dragged Casey off of the couch and out the front door with Rusty barking in circles at their feet.

"Oh, Janie, it's fantastic! It's so sleek and the color makes it look so, I don't know, expensive and dignified." They both giggled.

"Well, do ya want to go for a ride?" Janie asked, wanting to break in her new bike.

"Sure! I just need a few minutes first. Gotta take Rusty for a short walk."

"Yeah? I'll go with you." So the girls went for a quick walk with him. Rusty loved to mark every tree he came to and made fancy little circles when he was up to serious business.

"Man," Janie said, "I'll never get used to the cute dancing little dogs do when they're about to poop." The girls laughed. Rusty stood still and gave them a firm glare.

"Look at him," Casey said. "I actually think he prefers we turn our heads while he's busy."

"Sorry, Rusty!" They said in unison.

After they'd said their good-byes to their fluffy little friend, they hopped on their bikes and took off toward the park, knowing they'd have to rush it to get plenty of riding in before it got too dark to be on bikes.

"You know what, Casey? I think all of the bad stuff is behind us now, don't you?"

Casey considered this, knowing some important things remained unexplained, like Tina's killer and who stole the bike.

Regardless, she said, "Yeah, I think we're doing fine!"

Once onto the bike trail, Janie sped up. "Race ya!" She challenged, and began pedaling as fast as she could, but Casey was soon right behind her.

They reached the pond before slowing.

"Hey there," Janie shouted out to Mr. Curtis.

Mr. Curtis seemed to glare at the girls, but Janie assumed it was simply because the sun was in his eyes. They pedaled closer to him.

"Well, hello there, Janie dear. What's this, a new bike? That's certainly a big surprise." He gave a tired and wary smile in her direction. He then nodded to Casey.

"Oh yes, my dad just bought it for me. Isn't it great?" She grinned with pride.

There was no mention that her old bike had been stolen, although they imagined that he probably knew about it from Casey's mother or from someone else in the community. Everyone quickly knew all of the important news in Candice Bay.

He patiently let the girls chatter about the specifications of this particular bicycle model. While he wiped sweat from his face with his towel, Mr. Curtis said, "Hey, how about it if I get you a nice yellow vest that illuminates so you can safely wear it when riding at night?" With less interest in his voice and as a side note, he added, "I could get one for you, too, Casey."

The girls looked at each other, knowing they'd never wear something so ugly. Together they cheerily responded, "No thank you!"

Janie added, "But that was really nice of you to offer!"

Before Mr. Curtis could say anything else, they sped off.

"Oh, can you just imagine me wearing a yellow vest with this new bike?" Janie said.

Casey corrected Janie, "You mean, an ILLUMINATED yellow vest!" They both laughed harder.

Mr. Curtis's clenched jaw twitched, and he turned away before they could realize that he had heard them.

During the evening, Casey had another tutoring session with Adam. They had been seeing each other at least weekly since Mark introduced them.

After an hour of serious study and review, Adam suggested, "Casey, let's take a break, okay?"

"Sure," Casey responded, "it's up to you how much we work." She smiled while she pat his hand.

They closed their books and put their supplies up. He smiled at Casey, gently touching her face, leaned in, and gave her a gentle kiss on her cheek.

"Again," Casey said, giggling. And he gave her a sprinkling of kisses on her face, nose, and neck.

Casey quickly turned to cause him to kiss her on the lips. First gently, then more passionately while they embraced.

Suddenly they heard Casey's mother open the back door. The couple sat up straight.

Adam whispered, "We'll have to go somewhere else for our next study."

"No kidding!" Casey responded.

They planned to study at the library again, and go to a movie at the local theater afterward. It would be their first date.

In early August, Janie approached her parents about Jake.

"So that's why you've been acting so silly lately," her mother responded, laughing. "You have a boyfriend."

Her dad thoughtfully replied, "You've been through so much this year: losing a friend, being assaulted, having your bike vandalized, and then it was stolen. We just want you to be happy."

Her parents nodded to each other.

"Janie, you can spend some time with your boyfriend," her mother said. "But you must be reasonable. We want to get to know Jake. Okay?"

Janie happily agreed and they shared a group hug.

Within weeks, Jake and Janie were inseparable. One day Janie approached her parents again.

"Mom, Dad," Janie said, "Jake's family will be on

vacation for a week at the beach. They invited me to go along."

"Well," her dad responded, "my little girl is growing up." He thoughtfully looked to his wife to make this decision.

"You know we like Jake, and we like his parents. I'll want to talk with his mother about this and any details, but yes. Yes, you can go."

Janie was thrilled. "You're the best parents EVER!" she said, and she hugged and kissed each of them.

"Sweetheart," Janie's dad began, "we aren't going on a vacation any time soon. But let's plan on taking Jake with us to the river during Labor Day weekend, before school starts. Okay?"

"What a wonderful way to reciprocate," Janie's mother said.

They all agreed to invite Jake to the river with them.

During a cell conversation, Janie told Casey, "Well, it's not like I've abandoned you, because you have interests of your own."

"Yeah," Casey said, "where'd you hear that from?"

"Oh, I have my sources," Janie replied. "So tell me about Adam."

The girls giggled.

"Well, as you may know, Adam is a friend of Mark's, was in need of science tutoring for the summer, and since I do well in honors classes, Mark asked me if I wanted to help."

"Got it. Tell me more," Janie encouraged.

"Well, Adam's a year older than me, soon to get his learner's permit. He keeps good grades in all his subjects other than science. He plans to be a business major in college, and science is a required course. He wants to get at least a C in it."

Janie said, "I guess you were happy to accept the tutoring job since you can spend extra money on clothes and stuff for school."

"Yeah, sure," Casey said, "but when Mark introduced us, we were both so awestruck. He was so hot, and I could tell he felt that way about me. We've learned that we're a great match, both interested in sports, especially soccer and bike riding. The chemistry was right."

"What about Steve? Did you lose your interest in him?" Janie asked.

"Oh yeah. Steve." Casey paused. "He did speak to me after the graduation, but nothing afterwards. It's like he's not real. Just a fantasy. Adam is definitely real."

Casey smiled. "Yeah, Adam is so sweet, and very affectionate. He's a great kisser. We're a fantastic match."

"Oh, Casey, this is so wonderful!" Janie said enthusiastically. "We both have boyfriends!"

"Yeah," Casey said, "I think once school starts, our circle of friends will include Adam and Jake. We'll probably all ride together to and from school in Adam's car, once his parents get one."

"That sounds great," Janie said. "Do you know when Adam will get a car?"

"His parents already promised him it would be sometime in September," Casey said.

Janie paused. "Casey, it sure has been a very long summer when you consider Tina's death and everything.

We don't know any more about Tina's killer than at the beginning of the summer. Three months! When will this be resolved?"

Casey responded, "I think we might have to accept it that her murderer might never be known and never be punished." She continued, "But many great things happened during the summer too. Like your romance."

Janie giggled while Casey continued, "You are, after all, a most adorable couple.

"Thank you!" Janie said, "and you've found a fella that you really like."

"Yes, but we're just starting out, at a slow pace," Casey explained.

One morning in late August while the family sat at the kitchen table, Casey's dad was perusing the newspaper, "Well I see the Candice Bay Police Department has officially released the empty house as part of their murder investigation."

Casey's mom looked at the newspaper article. "Yes, I suppose this means much of the investigation has ended." She added, "well, the candlelight vigils had already ended."

"Life goes on, honey," Casey's dad said while he squeezed Casey's hand.

Casey nodded. "I know that, Dad,"

Casey's mother commented, "now I suppose the realtors can get that house back onto the market."

Mark laughed. "Yeah, well. I don't know how much luck they'll have in selling a house that a body was found in."

Casey's dad agreed. "You're right, son. Even if the buyers happened to come from a different area and were not aware of Tina's murder, the realtors are obligated to inform them."

Chapter 13

Before dusk, Janie left the house. She wandered along her street alone, kicking pebbles along her path.

She was deep in thought about whether she'd get her hair cut short or just get a trim when she went to the salon the next day. Several girls told her they liked the hair style she had, which took thirty minutes to prepare with the hot iron or hot curlers. She touched her hair, feeling the ends. She could tell that they were already getting dry and brittle.

After getting all sweaty in P.E. class, especially when playing soccer, it would be really hard to do anything with her hair. It would be so much more convenient to have it short, just to let her hair fall where it may after using good shampooing and conditioning products. That would mean less time every morning at the mirror and less work after P.E., and maybe even less sweat.

Janie's thoughts were interrupted when Mr. Curtis yelled to her from his porch. "Hey there Janie-gal. Come here a second, will ya? I have to tell you something." He paused, quickly licking his lips and nervously shoving his hands in and out of his pockets. "I figured out something about who took your bike."

Rallied with excitement and interest, Janie took only seconds to rush through the gate of the white picket fence toward his front porch.

Well, naturally it would be Mr. Curtis to solve this theft because he is such a kind and caring person and he's always watching out for me.

"Really? That's great news!"

She frowned for a moment once she'd caught up with him on the porch. "I've been so confused and concerned about this. I don't understand why someone would take my bike in the first place." She gazed into his eyes.

Mr. Curtis smiled kindly, holding the screen door open with one hand and the other hand reaching out to her. "Come dear. Come inside quickly. I don't want the neighbors to see that I'm the one telling you this."

He quickly added, "I have to watch my reputation, after all. Don't want to be known as a tattle-tale."

Without giving it a second thought, Janie let Mr. Curtis guide her through the doorway, and she heard the screen slam against the door frame behind her. He turned to latch the front door and then guided her past the couch and on toward the kitchen.

Funny, she thought, *we've never been to Mr. Curtis's house before, but he's been to ours several times.*

She impatiently stopped in the hallway between the living room and the kitchen and faced Mr. Curtis, saying, "Please tell me what you know! I can't wait to hear it."

Mr. Curtis calmly patted her hand. "Oh my dear, please don't rush me. Let me share the whole story with you over a cup of tea. Come dear, let's go into the kitchen and get comfortable."

Casey decided to give Rusty a much-needed bath outside on the patio using an oval-shaped bucket that the family uses for ice and drinks when they have dinner on the patio. Doing this on the patio was a bit awkward, since she usually bathes him in the bathtub. Rusty wiggled to free himself from her grip.

"Stop it, Rusty!" she fussed.

After a minute of continued whining from him, she said, "You'll be out of here in no time."

Rusty whimpered while Casey lifted him out of the bucket. "There, all done. I just have to dry you off." But while she began to dry his feet, Casey accidently pulled one of his front toenails back too far. Rusty growled and nipped at her.

Before giving it more thought, she rapped him on the nose, "NO!" she yelled, while looking into his eyes. "You don't dare growl or bite me!" Then she firmly carried him into the house, and as soon as she set him down, he ran into the living room.

Well this is crap! She muttered to herself. *All these years and I have my first fight with my best friend.* She looked at the mess she'd made. *I should've taken him to the bathtub, like I always do. Then this wouldn't have happened.*

Casey dumped the water near the shrubbery and threw the dog shampoo and conditioner into the bucket. She then wrung the wet wash cloth. She threw it and the towel into the bucket as well. While Casey propped the back door open to carry the bucket inside, Rusty ran out the door by her feet.

"Rusty! Stop!" she yelled. But he continued to run.

Casey quickly put the bucket down. *Oh my God! He'll get lost!* She immediately began running after him. "Rusty, stop!"

Mark's Mustang was parked at the front of the house, where he and Joey were working under the hood. They looked up to see Rusty, and then Casey run past them.

"Oh shit! Rusty's loose," Mark said.

Joey looked up, "yeah?"

"Come on, let's go," Mark said. They both took off running in the direction that Rusty and Casey had gone.

Joey asked, "Won't he come home on his own?"

"I don't know. He's never run off like this."

Just then they saw Casey cut into a neighbor's yard and go around to the back of it. They followed. They had already lost sight of Rusty. Casey continued to cut through another neighbor's back yard, and stopped.

"Rusty!" she slowed down and began to cry. Mark and Joey caught up with her.

"Where is he?" Mark asked, while they all looked around frantically. There was no sign of him anywhere. Casey continued to cry and Joey hugged her, trying to comfort her.

Mark said, "Let's think about this a minute. Where would he go? Where do you take him when you walk him, Casey?"

Casey wiped her face with her hand. "I guess, most often when we're this far, we're walking to Janie's."

"Okay then. Let's do that. We'll walk her street. Walk fast, but don't run." He looked at Casey and at Joey, "Once every few minutes, Casey will yell for him." He looked at his sister, "Say something calmly like, 'come here Rusty,' so he'll come to you instead of run further."

"Okay."

"Sounds like a plan," agreed Joey.

So Casey, Mark and Joey began their walk to Janie's street, with Casey calling for Rusty.

Mr Curtis directed Janie to the table. She sat down and waited patiently while he prepared the tea with his back to her. They continued to chat until the tea kettle began whistling. He arranged a tray with a sugar bowl, filled the creamer and got out cups and saucers.

"Now here you go, my dear. Watch, it may be too hot," he said as he carefully placed a delicate tea cup and saucer set in front of her.

The design was pretty red and pink roses with a golden rim. *This setting probably belonged to his deceased wife. I remember he told us that she had died some time ago.*

"Oh, thank you, Mr. Curtis." Janie reached for the cup, but when she tried to lift it, she bumped the cup against the saucer and spilled some of the hot tea onto the table. Afraid she would get burned, Janie jumped up quickly, causing the entire cup to dump onto the floor. Although tea had flown everywhere, the cup and saucer lay on the table.

Mr. Curtis yelled, "Look what you've done!" He quickly caught himself and said, "I hope you haven't burned yourself."

Janie assured him that she had not burned herself. She apologized and offered to clean up the mess, but he would have none of that. After he'd cleaned the floor with an old towel, he threw it into the sink to drip and cool down.

He muttered in exasperation, "Well, so much for my special tea to help us along here."

She sat back down after he had cleaned up the mess.

Janie decided to stand up, but as she started to scoot the chair out from the table, she felt his hands push down hard onto her shoulders. "No, don't get up, stay right here for me."

She wasn't sure if she'd heard him right. He had never ordered her to do anything before and he sounded upset with her. *Is he mad? But it was only an accident! The tea cup and saucer weren't even broken, so this doesn't make sense.*

She turned to face him.

With his hands still firmly clamped on both of her shoulders, her gaze met his, and to her surprise and further confusion, she saw an unusual excitement in his eyes, an excitement that she'd never noticed before. It was odd. No creepy! No, it was just odd.

Oh, yeah, she thought. *He must be overly excited to be the one to solve this crime! That must be it, and of course he'd be eager to tell how he solved it. I'm just causing him to be impatient,* so she relaxed.

She looked again at his face, into his eyes. Their eyes

locked and time stood still.

While he continued to stare deep into her eyes, she realizes that these were not the eyes of her kind friend, but the eyes of a stranger. They were cold, dark holes penetrating into her, causing a chill to run up her spine.

These were the eyes of a man she'd never known and didn't want to know. Everything inside her yelled, *GET OUT! Get out NOW!*

Janie instinctively raised her arm, forcing herself free from his hands. Standing, she faced him now. She was not sure what he would do, but definitely felt she needed to be on the defensive.

She crouched with her arms stretched out. Every nerve and muscle in her body was alert and ready to take action.

To her horror, this man who until now had been a grand-fatherly figure, a kind and gentle person, this man whom she had trusted, seemed now to be an enemy. How utterly confusing!

Her thoughts flew to Tina, but she refused to let her body go numb from the fear and shock of it. *NO! I will FIGHT this.*

Janie turned and began to run, shoving the nearest chair and the kitchen table into his pathway.

Mr. Curtis lunged at her, grabbing her neck and shoulders. "What are you doing?" she yelled hysterically. She gained some distance back into the hallway toward the living room.

This is a short distance. I can do it. She looked back toward Mr. Curtis to gauge whether she could get free. She urged her body to move.

He continued grabbing at her, grasping a loop on the waist of her jeans. While they struggled he whispered in a calm, yet determined voice, "Don't run from me. You cannot get away."

Desperate, Janie glanced around her. She quickly saw furniture she could use to create obstacles in his path to help her reach the living room.

She gave him a mighty push, shoving him into his desk and chair, knocking him and the chair, and ripping the loop of her jeans that was still in his grasp. He fell to his knees while the chair fell to the floor on its side. It was a few seconds before he regained his balance.

While he threw himself at her, she darted into the opposite direction, thankful now for the many times she had maneuvered on the soccer field, vying with her opponents on the field for possession of the ball.

As she weaved just ahead of Mr. Curtis, getting past the couch and toward the doorway, she glanced out his picture window and saw her dear friend, Casey, with Mark and Joey walking past the house.

Praise God! She screamed in the loudest, sharpest voice she'd ever heard: "CASEY! HELP ME! Help me NOW!"

Casey, Mark, and Joey all heard the scream and stopped immediately.

"What the hell was that?" Mark asked.

"I don't know. It sounded like Janie's voice," Casey said.

Joey added, "Yeah. And she said your name."

They looked around, confused. They couldn't see

Janie anywhere.

Joey wrinkled his brow. "I think it came from inside somewhere. Like, that house right there."

Mark agreed, "That's where I think it came from, too." He paused, "and it makes sense. We're right in front of the picture window. She must've seen us."

Frightened for Janie, Casey said hysterically, "We've gotta do something. I mean now!"

Joey was the first to approach the house; he opening the gate and proceeded to the porch. The others followed him.

Mr. Curtis clamped a hand across her mouth, wrestled her to the floor, and held her down with the sheer weight and force of his body. Now beet-red with anger and the tremendous physical labor this attack required, he pressed his face against hers. "You will pay DEARLY for this! I told you, you can NOT get away from me!" His spit hit her cheeks and nose.

Janie sent out silent prayers.

Unable to move from his grasp, she began to fill with regret as she realized how naïve she had been to trust and allow this man to so easily trap her in his house.

Mom and Casey both tried to warn me to be careful.

Defeated, she cried, knowing she might die, just like Tina. His hand was still firmly clamped over her mouth.

Mr. Curtis whispered his ugly and nasty plans for her young, limp body.

The screen door screeched, and they heard Casey. "Janie, are you all right?"

Immediately Mark asked, "What's goin' on?"

One of them knocked at the door.

Janie struggled, but she could not make a sound.

Janie's friends listened for a few seconds, and then Joey said, "The hell with this! Help me break the door down. Go!" Together, he and Mark hit the door with the force of their bodies.

There was a loud thud, and the front door burst open. The hinges broke and wood splinters flew.

Mr. Curtis let go of his grasp as he moved off of Janie, looking up at them, his angry face now a mixture of hatred and defeat. He held hatred toward these strong young men and Casey. She had always been a hindrance to his efforts to catch Janie alone. The hatred was also held toward his victim and most especially toward himself for being so stupid to get caught. If only the spiked tea had not been spilt, he could have maneuvered Janie with ease.

Realizing he was now at their mercy, he slowly sat up. Janie jumped up and rushed to her friends.

Casey held out her arms to Janie. "Oh My God, Janie! Are you all right?" She quickly gave Janie a visual check. "You have several bruises." Casey's eyes teared.

Janie attempted to respond, "I. Uh. I." She squeezed Casey's arms while sobs began to flow. She gasped, "He killed Tina. Wanted to kill me!"

"Come on, Janie. Let's get far away from this crazy house!"

While Casey and Janie ran out into the yard, Joey and Mark remained, blocking the door so Mr. Curtis could not make any movement toward the girls. They stood tall, determined and ready to fight.

Facing him, the boys stayed in the foyer. Mark pulled out his cell phone and dialed 911 while Joey leaned his hand onto Mr. Curtis, saying, "I think you're in real big trouble now, Perv!"

With a sinister smile, Joey asked, "So what're you gonna do now?"

Mr. Curtis remained frozen, unable to decide what to do next. He was enraged. He alternately muttered and yelled as if he were insane. "After all my patience and careful planning! My Janie belongs to ME!"

He slumped over and stared at the floor. Almost in tears, he said, "I'm just a stupid old man. They beat me."

Mr. Curtis glared at Mark and Joey, and rallied his anger again. "Damn! They caught me in the act, in my home! Now I'm nothing. NOTHING!" He hated them. He hated himself.

Mr. Curtis managed to pull himself off the floor, and he remained standing in place. He continued to glare at the young men. "Sons of bitches. Destroyed my entire future!" His hands clenched into tight fists.

The girls stood at the end of the sidewalk, just inside the gate to Mr. Curtis's house. Janie cried pitifully while Casey held her in her arms and dusk settled in around them. Curious neighbors crowded the street, congesting the pathway for the three police cars that honked and flashed their lights as they proceeded to Mr. Curtis's house.

Within moments of assessing the events that happened at Mr. Curtis's house, two officers came for Mr. Curtis. Relieved that they no longer had to stand guard over him, Mark and Joey stood silently near the police car, watching a very tired and sad old man, Mr. Curtis, being quietly placed into the back seat of a patrol car, with his hands cuffed behind him.

After an hour had passed, Janie's parents arrived home from their routine grocery shopping. They looked up the street and saw the crowd of neighbors and police cars on their block. They parked and rushed to the scene, worried for their neighbors.

"Oh my, honey," Janie's mother yelled to her husband, "They're at Mr. Curtis's house! I think something may've happened to Mr. Curtis!"

They managed to quickly move through the crowd to their daughter and Casey. Both girls were crying.

"Is Mr. Curtis okay?" Janie's mother asked. While her parents held Janie close, Casey quickly shared what she, Mark, and Joey had walked into.

"Are you serious?" Janie's dad yelled, "Bastard!" he let go of Janie and began to head toward where Mr. Curtis was. He glared ahead and shoved a couple of people out of his way.

His wife ran up to him, grabbed his arm while blocking him, "Honey. Stop." She looked into his eyes and calmly told him, "Let the police handle this. We need to take care of Janie."

He slumped and looked at the ground, and nodded his head. They returned to Casey and Janie. Shortly after, an officer came over to them.

"Excuse me, Are you Janie's or Casey's parent's? I'm Officer Trent." He held his hand out to shake their hands.

"Janie's our daughter, Officer," responded Janie's dad. "I don't think Casey's parents are here. I don't see them."

The officer looked at his tablet that he was carrying. He looked at Janie, still quietly crying into her mother's chest, and decided maybe he should leave Janie with her mother for a while longer. "I would like to borrow Casey for a few minutes, just to get a brief preliminary statement from her."

Janie's dad nodded his head, "Okay, if that's what you gotta do. We certainly want to cooperate in this."

The officer added, "Yes. We'll need to get Janie's preliminary statement too, in a few minutes." He paused, "We'll also need Janie and her friends to go to the police station tonight for interviews, with the parents."

Janie's dad nodded again, "I'll call Casey's parents now." He began dialing into his cell while the police officer escorted Casey to his patrol car.

Janie's dad reached Casey's parents. They had been at the hardware store, picking out a few more flower pots to place on their front porch. Once he had shared with them the shocking news, Casey's parents rushed to meet the others at Janie's house.

While traveling, Casey's mom called Joey's parents, and they arrived at Janie's house soon afterward.

Once everyone was assembled in the living room, Janie's dad suggested, "Folks, I believe that Janie, Casey, Mark, and Joey should each tell their story to us before they go to the station tonight."

Casey's dad nodded, "Yes, I certainly agree on that."

Joey's dad looked at the teenagers, "Yes. It could serve as practice before they formally give their statements to the police."

Joey's mother added, "I just want to hear it all now, so I can wrap my head around it."

"I know what you mean. It's all so shocking!" said Casey's mother.

Janie's mother nodded agreement, while she held her daughter close.

As Janie tried to tell her story, her parents were shocked to hear the details of how their trusted friend had attacked their daughter. Mr. Curtis had fooled them. When she had finished, the group sat in silence.

Joey's mother then asked, "How could this happen?"

Casey's mother responded, "This simply re-emphasizes our earlier question when we learned that Tina had been killed: How can we trust any of our neighbors again?"

Janie's father said, "Thank God he didn't harm you, and that your friends came when they did."

Janie's mother hugged her daughter, "I shudder to imagine what would've happened to you if it had not been for your friends passing by to hear your cry for help."

Casey's dad held his forehead with his hand, "Surely

God looked down and sent angels to protect her." He paused. "This evil crime committed in our beautiful community will affect everyone here."

"Yes," Janie's mother agreed, "it's forever tainted. But we have our Janie. Thank God!"

Casey's mom sighed, looking at her husband. "Regardless. I guess it will be a long time before folks can recover from the deeds of that horrible man."

Casey suddenly jumped up. "Oh my God! I forgot about Rusty!"

"Rusty?" her mother asked.

"Yes, mom, he's lost! He ran away! That's why we were walking by Mr. Curtis's house in the first place, to find him."

Before Casey reached further panic, Joey's mother waved her hands, interrupting, "No, no Casey. Rusty is not lost. He's at our house."

"What?"

"Yeah, I was going to let you all know, but I forgot with all this happening." She looked at the group. "We went out the door to meet with everyone, and there he was, lying on the front porch, obviously exhausted."

Joey's dad added, "So we just put him in the house, and left him there, and we took the twins to Mrs. Pitchford's house, next door, to babysit them."

Casey smiled, "Oh thank God! I was so worried about him." She looked at Mark and Joey, "Thank you for trying to help me."

Mark gave her a gentle slug on her arm, "At least we got our exercise."

Joey laughed, "Yeah, right."

Casey's dad pursed his lips, "I don't believe it was a mere coincidence that these teens happened to be right at Mr. Curtis's house to hear Janie scream for their help." He shook his head, "No. That was a God thing."

The rest of the parents agreed. Janie's dad added, "Praise God! Thank you Jesus!" he held his hands out, and one by one, the group held hands in a circle for prayer.

Chapter 14

During the next several weeks, while Mr. Curtis waited for his day in court, Janie remained fearful, so she and her friends kept close tabs on one another's whereabouts. Out of curiosity, or maybe as an effort to regain courage, Janie persuaded Casey to walk by Mr. Curtis's house with her.

Concerned, Casey asked, "Janie, are you sure you can do this? I mean, you seem to be getting over what happened pretty good. I just don't want your progress to stop."

Janie kicked a few small pebbles away with her foot, "I believe this might be a part of my moving on."

"Okay, as long as you're sure."

They began to slowly walk away from Janie's house, toward Mr. Curtis's house. The yellow security tape was still in place, since police had not completed their investigation of the crime scene. Just as they began to pass the bushes at the edge of her own property, Janie stopped.

"Casey, how do you do it?" she hesitated, looking to the ground to give herself time to think it through before continuing. "This is hard for me to admit, but I know I'm not strong and confident like I should be, like you are, and I want to be. Mr. Curtis was at least partly able to fool me because I was naive. I didn't have warning instincts about him and I'm certainly not courageous, like you seem to be." She sighed. "Can you help me, you know, get there?"

"But you do have instincts of your own. You just need to be more willing, and more confident to listen to them." They continued to stand at Janie's property edge.

"Instincts?" Janie responded.

"Yeah. It's like little warning whispers that God gives you. Do you remember ever being in a situation, and you suddenly felt uncomfortable, like having a feeling of dread? Or you had a bad feeling about someone, but couldn't pin-point what it was that bothered you? Maybe they said or did something that you felt your conscious checked about?" Casey asked.

Janie shook her head, "I don't know, let me think about that...Probably, if I did have little warning signals going off inside me, I quickly shot them down. I was more interested in pleasing other people." Janie cupped her hand to her mouth, "What do you mean about my conscious being checked?"

"Hmmm. Let me give you an example. If I asked you to go into a store with me to be the lookout, so I could steal something, you'd immediately feel fluttering going on inside. Maybe you'd even have a conflict going on for a few seconds, because I'm your friend. But you know you couldn't live with yourself if you went along with such a plan."

Janie smiled, "Okay, I think I understand. I do have instincts happening sometimes, and my conscious does get checked." Janie's voice lowered, "I had feelings like that when we lived in New York sometimes. Like once, I remember walking into a small shop along my street while a few men were inside talking. I had been in there several times before with no problems. But that time, once I stepped inside the door, I suddenly wanted to get out. I quickly left, too. Later I wondered what might've been wrong. Maybe a robbery was about to happen, or maybe I had interrupted a drug deal in-process."

They slowly moved further toward Mr. Curtis's house by several feet.

Casey stopped walking and put her hand on Janie's shoulder, "Wait a minute. Remember how good you felt when you spoke up to Butch? That took courage. You weren't ugly, but it was something negative for him to hear. It had to be said."

Janie smiled, "Yeah. It was hard to say, but I felt good about it. "

They continued to walk, and picked up their pace.

Casey patted her friend's shoulder. "You had courage while you fought for your life. We both know and have a confidence that God is watching over us. And, He must have been with you for you to get away from Mr. Curtis."

"That's so true," Janie said, smiling at Casey.

Casey looked upward, "I think it is appropriate to remember this verse I've heard my great Aunt

Grace recite several times to my Granny, 'Have not I commanded thee? Be strong and of good courage: be not afraid, neither be thou dismayed; for the Lord thy God is with thee whithersoever thou goest.' It's in Joshua 1, verse 9, in the King James' Bible."

Janie quickly agreed, filled with faith. "Yes, I do know that whatever may happen, it can't be bigger than God is."

She paused. "But, is it so wrong to choose to look at the good in people?"

Casey quickly responded, "Janie, that is a gift you have. We're supposed to look for the good in others, but that's hard to do when you know about bad stuff going on...Janie, many people really like you just the way you are."

"Yeah, I know there's been times when I just wanted to make everyone happy with me, and I went out of my way to please them. But I didn't feel used. Really, I enjoyed it."

Casey said, "Maybe you're just having a hard time figuring out where to draw the line between being a nice, helpful person, and then going so far that you're pleasing people to the extent that it's a great expense to you."

Janie considered what Casey had said. "Yes. I did that with the candy for the band. I was trying to please Jake and his band friends. The time I spent on that project took away from my homework. Even while I was working on getting sales, I knew Jake cared about me anyway. I didn't need to work on selling the candy so much."

Casey smiled, "Yeah, and I went too far trying to help you sell candy while I knew I should be spending that time on my science project. It was not easy to make up for the time lost. I'm just saying I go too far to please people sometimes, too."

Janie paused, "Well, Casey, I want you to know that I'm seeing a counselor to help me get over the trauma. She says it will take me some time. She is also trying to help me build my self-esteem and to learn to build boundaries when I want to help others."

"Everything's going to be fine, isn't it?" They smiled and laughed out loud when they realized that they had walked past Mr. Curtis's house without noticing while they were talking.

The Police Department's investigation of the crime scene was first performed by their forensic team. They gathered fingerprints, took many crime scene photographs, and obtained any items that they felt may be useful in the investigation. Once their work was completed, they returned to the Police Department's forensic laboratory for further work on their findings.

Investigator Howard and Officers Evans and Tillet were assigned to investigate the crime scene for crime trophies, journals, letters, and anything they felt was evidence in building their case against Mr. Curtis.

Investigator Howard and the officers each put their plastic gloves on, and they carried packages of baggies to place samples in. Once on Mr. Curtis's porch, Officer Evans opened the door and the men entered the living room with deliberate, but careful steps.

Investigator Howard glanced into the coat closet. The top shelf was cluttered. "Officer Tillet, be sure to go through everything up here, and I want you to check inside each coat pocket, and inside each shoe and boot before we pass on the closet."

"Yes sir," replied Officer Tillet. "I can check every closet in the house if you like."

"Sure," responded Investigator Howard, while he moved on to review the top of a desk in the corner. "Officer Evans, I'd like you to check all the drawers here, and furniture."

Officer Evans quickly responded, "Already on it, sir."

Officer Evans noticed Investigator Howard moving toward the kitchen area. "I'll handle the kitchen area as well."

"Okay," responded Investigator Howard. He paused at the entrance to the kitchen. "I understand forensics found what they believe to be rohypnol in the kitchen cabinet."

"Well that certainly goes along with the victim's account that it seemed to trigger Mr. Curtis's change when she spilled the tea he had given her," said Officer Evans.

"Date rape drug," added Officer Tillet. "Yeah. Maybe Mr. Curtis would've been successful if she hadn't spilled it."

"That little girl is very fortunate for that accident. And for her friends to come along when they did," responded Investigator Howard.

"Angels must've been looking out for her," said Officer Tillet, while he reached into the last boot in the coat closet. "Nothing here, sir." He closed the closet door and moved on to his next task.

Investigator Howard had walked through the kitchen area, then came back into the living room. "Okay. After you two finish the bedroom, and the bath, then come join me in the basement," Investigator Howard said.

"Got it," replied Officer Evans. Officer Tillet nodded agreement and headed toward the hallway leading to the bedroom.

Once in Mr. Curtis's basement, Investigator Howard glanced around the entire area and rested his eyes upon Mr. Curtis's bookcase which had two shelves filled with black, leather-bound journals. *Well, what have we here,* he mused.

Inspector Howard pulled the first journal from the higher shelf and began leafing through the pages. He quickly sat it down and pulled another journal, glanced through it, and then pulled one from the lower shelf to review.

Very interesting. Investigator Howard brought the first journal with him to the nearest chair, turned on the lamp, and began to read it.

Soon Officers Evans and Tillet came down the steps to join him. "Found anything?" asked Officer Tillet. He glanced at Investigator Howard reading a journal and noticed the other journals.

Officer Evans walked to the bookshelf and began looking through one of the journals.

"Yes, it appears Mr. Curtis liked to make a detailed account of his plans and bad actions," said Investigator

Howard.

Both officers picked up several journals and began to peruse them. After a few minutes, Officer Tillet said, "Oh my! He's provided quite a meticulous record here."

"For sure," added Officer Evans. "It's not like he can now say that his actions weren't premeditated."

Investigator Howard selected another journal, and placed it into his lap, then looked up at his men. "Mr. Curtis described his patient efforts to win the trust of the community while he performed various volunteer roles."

"Wow. How cunning," said Officer Tillet. "I suppose he also recorded how he planned to gain Janie's and her parents' confidence, too."

"Yes. Always a pattern of starting with the parents." Investigator Howard paused. "We have a serial killer here."

"Geez," said Officer Evans, "the man looked like he could be a nice grandfather."

"That's a great part of the deception," said Office Tillet. "It's like his disguise, so you can't easily discern his intentions."

Investigator Howard said, "Well boys, from what I've seen so far, these journals began about ten years ago, the same year that his wife died in Vermont."

"Guess that may be when it all started," said Officer Evans. He paused. "Did you notice he says 'we' sometimes? I wonder if he had a partner."

"That's what I've been thinking, too. But I don't see anyone else named." Investigator Howard paused.

"Regardless, Mr. Curtis seemed to take the credit for it all. Guess he was the man in charge."

About that time Officer Tillet said, "Oh man! We've hit the jackpot now. Just look at all of this!"

"Oh, you've found the trophies," said Officer Evans. "We found nothing of concern upstairs, so I figured they would be here."

Investigator Howard quickly reviewed the items. "I wonder just how many unsolved crimes these will connect to." He looked at his men. "Let's pack up all of this and get to the department."

Once at the Police Department, Investigator Howard and the officers met with Officer Brown, who had been gathering information about Mr. Curtis by surfing the internet. Officer Brown was very interested in the journals and trophies that were found at Mr. Curtis's house.

Officer Brown shared his findings. "Mr. Curtis wasn't even his real name. His real name was Curtis Dunn, and there was an outstanding warrant against him for attempted assault on a minor in Vermont. He was a person of interest in the homicide of another minor. Now the law enforcement in Virginia and those in Vermont are sharing information and both have been investigating for more information on Mr. Dunn."

Investigator Howard asked, "So what else do you have?"

Officer Brown pulled up a photo on his website for the men to see. "Obviously, his appearance changed greatly during the past decade. He used to be obese, weighing over three-hundred pounds, and he wore a mustache and beard."

"Whew. Good disguise. He looks entirely different," commented Officer Evans.

"Yeah. At today's arrest, I'd bet he didn't even weigh one-eighty. He was fairly muscular for a sixty-four year-old man," said Officer Tillet.

"And, no facial hair. He was bald!" added Officer Evans.

The investigator asked Officer Brown, "How did they discover his true identity? DNA sampling's not had time. Fingerprints?"

"Yeah. Mostly fingerprints and process of elimination for certain parameters—you know, race, sex, approximate age range, and so on. Once the population was narrowed down some, we also used our new facial recognition program," responded Officer Brown.

"Well now. I think we've gathered a lot of indisputable evidence during such a short time. I feel confident that we can establish guilt beyond a reasonable doubt. And Mr. Dunn should be found guilty for Tina's death," said Investigator Howard.

"We're in agreement," said Officer Brown.

Investigator Howard continued, "The Department didn't reveal to the public that Tina had been tortured before she received the fatal blow to her head." He paused. "We found a shovel in the basement with a substance on it that I believe will prove to be her blood. Probably with his fingerprints, too. Most incriminating; most likely the murder weapon."

"Undoubtedly, the shovel was preserved as a trophy," added Officer Evans.

Investigator Howard and Officers Evans and Tillet left the Department to get a few hours of sleep, after working on the case essentially all night.

During the following afternoon, the men resumed their work, and began receiving some information from the forensics laboratory.

Investigator Howard said, "To sum it up with what we have so far, we found that Mr. Dunn's journal recorded numerous misdeeds that he was responsible for against Tina, and he detailed many torturous abuses she had suffered while being held captive for hours before her murder." He paused to look at the officers surrounding him. "It appears the only question for the judge and jury would be whether the death sentence or life imprisonment without parole will be imposed."

Inspector Howard continued, "There was ample physical evidence at Mr. Dunn's home and from witnesses that he, in fact, did kidnap and assault Janie. He lured her to his house under false pretenses. He physically restrained her." Investigator Howard paused to take a drink of coffee that someone handed him.

"According to Janie's testimony of his statements to her," Investigator Howard continued, "Mr. Dunn described his intentions for Janie to suffer and die as well."

The officers nodded their agreement to the information presented.

Officer Brown responded, "I believe that the prosecuting attorney's desire will be to show enough similarities to paint Mr. Dunn as a serial killer; but at this time, we don't have sufficient evidence, at least not in the Commonwealth of Virginia." He paused. "'Course, investigation's still in the beginning stages, and we already have much support."

Officer Evans said, "Following this state's judgment against Mr. Dunn for Tina's murder, because murder trumps assault or attempted murder, Mr. Dunn should then face charges in Janie's case and potentially for crimes committed in Vermont."

"If justice is served," added Officer Tillet, "that man will never be free."

"So far, Mr. Dunn has refused to talk, and he lawyered up," said Officer Brown.

"That's okay," said Investigator Howard. "Our investigation will continue, and any trial dates will be set for next year."

Officer Sands had been one of several officers in the office who stopped to listen to the discussion about the Mr. Dunn case. She also brought fresh coffee to the desks of the leading officers in this case.

Officer Sands said, "I live in the same community as Mr. Dunn, on the same street. I can say this: The terrible fate that befell Tina should never be forgotten, especially by her fellow students and friends." She paused to look at each officer in the room. "Plus this near-miss with Janie. It should bring our entire community together. I'm sure the churches, schools, and neighborhoods all are now keenly aware of what could happen."

Officer Evans interrupted, "You're right Officer Sands. Most communities have had mechanisms in place to ensure the safety of their citizens. With this history in mind, Candice Bay should demonstrate a renewed emphasis for safety."

Within a month of Mr. Dunn's arrest, police officers began coming to the area schools to give regular lectures on crime awareness. P.E. opened courses for self-defense lessons. Parents pledged to take additional steps to ensure the safety of their teens. Neighbors volunteered to buddy up and look out for each other through their neighborhood watch organization.

The lives of the small community had been rocked that summer in Candice Bay. They once thought nothing bad could touch them, but with this horrible event, they started thinking more about protecting citizens for the future.

Chapter 15

"Hey Mom, do you realize it's almost a year to the day since Tina disappeared?" Casey asked while she looked into her mother's eyes and held her hand. "I'm mentioning this because I think we need to take a break from all this. Do you think so?"

"Yes dear. Do you have something in mind?"

"Well, spring break is very near." Casey paused, not sure how to proceed.

Her mother laughed. "Your brother has already asked me about using our timeshare at Virginia Beach, and your father and I believed it was a great idea."

"Should have known!" Casey said, and they both laughed.

"Mark just needed to plan ahead. He had to ask for time off from work so he could join you and your friends for a few days," Casey's mother explained. "Plus, your father and I needed to know in plenty of time to make plans to be there. We will be watching over you and the other teens, you know."

"I didn't think about that," Casey said.

Once they had arrived at the Virginia Beach timeshare, just before dusk, the group of teens prepared for their evening by a bonfire on the beach. The weather was perfect, warm, but with a slight breeze. The ocean continually sent gentle waves to splash against the sandy beach, and then rolled back for the next wave. The teens carried to within feet of the water's edge their supplies for their bonfire: driftwood to feed the fire, beach chairs, blankets, driftwood to sit on, drinks packed in ice chests, and various snacks.

Adam brought his guitar and began quietly strumming a peaceful tune. Casey smiled. "Oh Adam, that sounds really nice."

Mark looked around at the group and asked, "Hey, has anyone ever heard from Butch after he and his family moved to Arizona?"

Joey said, "Well, you know more than I do about it; I didn't know Arizona was where they went. Who do they know there?"

"I heard him talking to his buddies about going there to visit his uncle's family one Christmas," Casey said, "I wonder what will become of him anyway?"

"Oh, I think he'll probably become a famous and wealthy business owner someday, and we will all read about him in the paper," Casey's boyfriend Adam said. They all laughed, and others agreed.

Janie carefully asked Casey, "Well, did anyone ever say anything to you about Marla Sims? I always hoped that she'd eventually be able to get herself together."

Casey looked sadly at her friend. "My mom called the assistant principal a few times about her, and although she wasn't allowed to give any details, apparently Marla is not doing much better yet. It's going to take her a lot of time to get through her problems and the cutting."

No one else wanted to comment about Marla. Some of them felt guilty for the ugly way they had treated her. The fire danced around the burnt wood, and sent tiny red cinders up into the air.

"Oh," said another girl. "You won't believe this! Guess who was arrested last week for shop lifting?" The group looked at one another, but none had heard about the incident. "Well, you may not know about it because her parents paid to keep it all hush-hush. It was Marcia!"

"Marcia?" Casey said. "What did she steal that she doesn't already have?"

"It was a sweater from Macy's. I only know because my mom works at the courthouse."

"Geez, I guess that was a real embarrassment for her family," said another.

The teens heard a loud crack as the wood shifted. Jake took a nearby stick and punched the pile of driftwood a few seconds. "Yeah, you just never know who's gonna commit such a crime. It doesn't seem to matter how well off they may be," Jake said thoughtfully.

Others agreed, while one girl reminded them of how snobby Marcia always had been.

"Yeah," said another, "she always looked down her nose at everybody. I guess she got hers."

That reminded all of them about the P.E. fight.

"You know, I was really impressed to find out about

Tish," said Joey's girlfriend, Cathy. "I didn't even know she could sing!"

Another girl said, "She's found God and really turned herself around. You know, she also sings regularly at our church now. Her voice is beautiful!"

"Oh yeah, she's changed big time!" Casey said. "I always knew there was a lot of good in that girl!" She and Janie smiled at each other.

Janie leaned over and whispered to Casey, "Girl, I'm gonna break you in half." They laughed, happy that they could now kid about it.

The group continued to reminisce about various friends and events at school that went on during the year, and talked about the improvements they had noticed in Candice Bay. Some of them brought up tidbits of gossip they'd heard.

"Hey, did you hear about ol' Mr. Stable getting together with the assistant principal?" someone said.

Another asked, "What? He's about ten years older than her."

Still another said, "But I thought she was married?"

"Man, you're way off." Joey said. "Her husband died about four years ago."

Cathy said, "Well, I'm just happy for her that she found someone, and age shouldn't matter so much."

"Aw, you're just sayin' that because Joey's older than you!" said one of the guys, and they all laughed at Cathy's expense.

Joey came over and hugged her, "Now lay off my sweetie, will ya?"

The guy came back with, "Oh we're just teasin'. You

two make a cute couple, that's all."

After a few moments, there was silence while each person quietly reflected.

Finally Jake spoke. "Well, I'm really thankful that my Janie here was rescued by our local heroes." His voice waivered while he looked upon them. "Thank you, man!"

Others added to it, "Oh yeah, that's for sure!" Some personally thanked each of them. The waves continued to peacefully splash against the sand.

Casey said, "I'm thankful that we happened along when we did, and I don't think for a second it was just by chance, either."

Another girl said, "Yeah, we need to thank the Lord that Janie was rescued, and that Dunn was caught."

A fella said, "Amen to that, sister. I hear you!"

Mark added, "May that animal rot in jail, too." Others agreed.

They all sat quietly; several of the teens stared into the small dancing flames against the embers.

In a soft voice, Casey prayed out loud, "Lord, we don't understand the *why's* in all that happened, but we know that Tina is now with you. Please continue to watch over her family, giving them peace and comfort. In Jesus name, Amen."

"Amen," said several of her friends. The group continued to sit still for another moment.

Suddenly someone cranked a boom box on and then turned the volume all the way up.

Another yelled, "Let's party!"

A couple of the girls used that as their cue to get

the food out, including the makings for s'mores. "Oh yeah, this is the life," yelled another teen, as he jumped up to grab someone to dance with.

Mark said, "Oh yeah! We know what it's like to go through bad times, and we sure can appreciate every happy moment now."

Casey added, "SPRING BREAK! Yeah, let's party!"

The Police Department had assigned Investigator Howard to the Dunn case originally, so he continued to represent the Police Department in the Virginia cases. He, in cooperation with the authorities in Vermont and other experts and prosecuting attorneys, continued the work on all of the related Dunn cases.

"One thing's for sure," Investigator Howard said to his officers, "we are all determined to get this man nailed." He paused. "The plan is to use a lesser sentence within Tina's case to encourage Mr. Dunn to come clean on the other incidents."

Officer Evans responded, "So we're holding the death sentence out as a way to gain cooperation, right?"

"That's right," said Investigator Howard.

"What's been puzzling me from the start is this: did Mr. Dunn act alone, or did he have a partner in crime?" asked Officer Evans. "It seems like with the more information we get, the more support we have that he didn't act alone."

Officer Tillet added, "Yeah. Findings from our computer geeks show that Mr. Dunn apparently met someone on the internet seven or more years ago, and that person apparently moved to Virginia around the same time he did, it would be logical to believe that person was either a friend likely aware of Mr. Dunn's actions, or someone working directly with him."

Investigator Howard nodded while he took a sip of hot coffee, then set the cup back onto his desk. "After reviewing all of our findings thus far, I believe Mr. Dunn's unidentified friend was an accomplice, and Vermont Investigators agree," said Investigator Howard. "Evidence tells us that Mr. Dunn and his buddy had been involved in Tina's and Janie's cases. We know that other person used an alias for several years, and it's just a matter of time until we have that person's identity."

"Yeah, but how much more time will it take?" asked Officer Evans. "You've already made several attempts to get Mr. Dunn to talk specifics, especially about this alleged accomplice, but with each interrogation, Mr. Dunn only joked and toyed with you" He paused. "Last time he openly laughed in your face."

Officer Tillet interjected, "Apparently Mr. Dunn feels that he has no further reason to mask himself as a kind old man. He doesn't have any hope for trial. So now the evil in him oozes out with his every word." He paused. "It was shocking though, when Mr. Dunn bragged about torturing Tina."

Investigator Howard said, "Mr. Dunn has chosen a rough route for himself. Here he is, now kept in solitary confinement while awaiting his trial date because several inmates threatened his life, mostly because of the types of crimes he'd done, but also because of the way he mocked the other prisoners."

"Yeah, he made it hard on himself," said Officer Evans. "And because Mr. Dunn refused to practice normal personal hygiene in prison, guards have had to occasionally spray him down." He paused. "And remember? When we searched his house, it was well organized. Fairly clean."

"He's just spiting himself now," agreed Officer Tillet.

Investigator Howard said, "Despite the prison conditions he has put on himself, we still believe that there's a chance to negotiate with him, since he does not want to face a death sentence."

One of the computer geeks from forensics, Roscoe, rushed into Investigator Howard's office. The men sat quietly, waiting for his news. Roscoe said, "Hey, we have a breakthrough coming from a cold case in Vermont that points to Mr. Dunn and an accomplice."

Roscoe paused. "You may recall that when our forensics team went through results of the female items found in Mr. Dunn's house, some items had sufficient DNA for testing. We shared our test results with Vermont. They matched the DNA of a Vermont teenage girl who was found dead five years ago. That case had remained an unsolved homicide until now." He paused and looked at the men. "Bottom line: There was additional DNA from a male, but it was not Mr. Dunn."

"Damn," announced Investigator Howard. "We have the accomplice's DNA."

Officer Evans smiled and said, "Yes!" He and Officer Tillet smacked each other's hands in a high-five.

Investigator Howard instructed Officer Evans,

"Evans, go set up our final interview with Mr. Dunn and his attorney, as well as the prosecuting attorney."

Vermont authorities had previously agreed, because of his experience and expertise in similar cases as Mr. Dunn's, and his specific knowledge in Mr. Dunn's cases, that Investigator Howard would conduct the interviews.

Investigator Howard looked across the table at Mr. Dunn in the interrogation room. He spoke concisely and firmly. "Mr. Dunn. We have a deal on the table. If you would provide the name of your accomplice and evidence connecting the accomplice to the case in Vermont and any in Virginia, then the Commonwealth has agreed to seek a sentence of only life imprisonment with no chance of parole." He paused. "No deals regarding any cases in Vermont are on the table. It would be up to Vermont to decide whether you still have to appear for trial on those."

Mr. Dunn seemed to enjoy the attention and caused the interview to drag along for hours, even though his attorney had initially stated that his client would be cooperative, and that he wanted to accept a deal that dropped the possibility of a death sentence.

During the last hour of the interview, Mr. Dunn finally began to get serious.

"Mr. Dunn, these are our final questions in this matter, and if you don't cooperate, the deal will go off the table. Did you or did you not participate in the events leading up to and including the kidnapping, assault, and murder of Tina Vanelli?" Investigator Howard began.

"Yes, I participated."

"Did you have anyone assisting you, whether directly or indirectly with the events leading up to and/or including the kidnapping, assault and murder of Tina Vanelli?"

"Yes."

"What evidence is there to prove you had an accomplice in the Tina Vanelli case?"

"My accomplice took some photos of Tina, just before she died and after, as trophies."

"Where are these photos?"

"I believe he keeps trophies in his garage."

"Did you participate, whether directly or indirectly in the events leading up to and/or including the kidnapping and assault of Janie Smith?" asked Investigator Howard.

"Yes, I participated."

"Did you have anyone assisting you, whether directly or indirectly, with the events leading up to and/or including the kidnapping and assault of Janie Smith?" Investigator Howard continued.

"Yes."

"What evidence is there to prove you had an accomplice in the Janie Smith case?"

"My accomplice has her bike, as a trophy." Mr. Dunn grinned.

"Where is the bike?"

"Like I said before, I believe he keeps trophies in his garage."

"How many, in total, accomplices did you have in the Tina Vanelli case, and in the Janie Smith case?" asked Investigator Howard.

"There was only one accomplice."

"What is the name of your accomplice in the Tina Vanelli and Janie Smith cases and where does he live and work?"

Resigned, Mr. Dunn answered, "William Thomason. He's a janitor at Candice Bay High School.

He's probably there right now. I don't recall his exact address, but he lives on Windsor Road. You should be able to look it up."

"Are you aware that this deal, to serve a life sentence with no parole and no death sentence for the Tina Vanelli case, and any action for the Janie Smith case is contingent upon the validity of your answers here?"

"Yes, I'm aware. Now go get my friend."

Before the interview ended, officers from the Candice Bay Police Department and the SWAT teams were deployed to Candice Bay High School and to what they identified as the home of William Thomason on Windsor Road.

The next morning, a Saturday, while Casey's family was gathered at the breakfast table, her dad announced, "Hey, here's something in the paper about Tina's case. Apparently they've found an accomplice!"

Everyone stopped to listen. "Please read the article to us, dear," urged Casey's mother.

"Sure," he responded, and cleared his throat to begin.

"During interrogation yesterday, Investigator

Howard reports that Mr. Dunn confessed to his actions in the kidnapping and murder of Tina Vanelli, and to his actions in the kidnapping and assault with intent to kill Janie Smith. He also confessed that he had an accomplice in both of these crimes."

"The accomplice!" Mark uttered.

"Oh my God. Please continue, dear," Casey's mother said.

Casey's dad straightened the paper, "Mr. Dunn named William Thomason, a janitor at Candice Bay High School, as his accomplice. Investigators were immediately dispatched to Mr. Thomason's residence, at 4402 Windsor Road.

"William our janitor?" Mark said, astonished.

Casey nodded, "I knew he was a creep."

Casey's mother interrupted her teenagers, "Shush! Let him finish the article!" She then nodded to her husband, encouraging him to continue reading.

"Investigators have found what appears to be crime-related trophies in Mr. Thomason's garage. The items included crime-scene photos of Tina Vanelli and a bicycle that matched the description of the stolen bike owned by Janie Smith."

Casey's dad looked up from the paper, saying, "All right, looks like they've got him good for this!" then he proceeded to read further.

"All items that appeared to relate to any Vermont cases were meticulously packed as evidence.

Because school had already let out, students were not there to witness the capture of their school janitor. The building was secured. Officers had been dispatched at every possible exit, while well-armed officers proceeded methodically into the building.

Mr. Thomason was mopping the first floor hallway when officers burst into the area. Mr. Thomason was apprehended without incident. Taken completely by surprise and without any weapons, he immediately surrendered."

"Man!" Mark interjected.

His dad continued, "During their investigation, police also found in the high school's basement, within the personal, locked desk drawer of Mr. Thomason's work bench, a large box containing only three red silk roses."

"What?" Casey said, with a wide-eyed expression.

Now that you've finished, please spread the word!

Tweet about the book
Share it on Facebook and Goodreads
Share the Amazon link and cover on Pinterest
Write a review on Amazon
Tell your friends
Contact the author with your thoughts

Find Carin Jayne Casey Online

Facebook: Carin Jayne Casey Author
Goodreads: Carin Jayne Casey
Amazon: Carin Jayne Casey

Website and Blog: CarinJayneCasey.com

About the Author

Carin Jayne Casey
Author

**Awareness. Compassion.
Recovery. Peace.**

The Lord is close to the broken hearted and saves those who are crushed in spirit.
{*Psalms 34:18 NIV*}

Carin Jayne Casey, the eldest of her siblings, grew up in a middle-class Ohio community. In the midst of parental dysfunction, she and her siblings enjoyed fun-filled childhood adventures. Her family moved from Ohio to rural West Virginia while she was a teenager.

Casey married her high-school sweetheart and bore two wonderful children. As with siblings, she encouraged her children to play imaginative games growing up. Her marriage failed, and she was eventually lured into a brief, violent relationship.

Casey strives to bring awareness of potential dangers to women while promoting spiritual growth. She believes adults should encourage children in healthy fun; children should be safe from harsh punishments; and families should practice appropriate consequences and forgiveness.

Casey graduated from Radford University in Virginia and is employed in risk management. As a survivor of domestic violence, she shares pathways to spiritual growth and recovery, assists women shelters, donates books, and participates in church missions. Casey and her husband have four children and six grandchildren.

Website: CarinJayneCasey.com
Email: CarinJayneCasey@gmail.com